THE ANDERSON FILES

THE ANDERSON FILES

The Unauthorized Biography of Gillian Anderson

Marc Shapiro

BOULEVARD BOOKS, NEW YORK

THE ANDERSON FILES:
THE UNAUTHORIZED BIOGRAPHY OF GILLIAN ANDERSON

A Boulevard Book / published by arrangement with the author.

PRINTING HISTORY
Boulevard edition / May 1997

For information address: The Berkley Publishing Group, 200 Madison Avenue, New York, New York 10016.

The Putnam Berkley World Wide Web site address is
http://www.berkley.com

ISBN: 1-57297-266-1

BOULEVARD
Boulevard Books are published by The Berkley Publishing Group, 200 Madison Avenue, New York, New York 10016.
BOULEVARD and its logo are trademarks belonging to Berkley Publishing Corporation.

PRINTED IN THE UNITED STATES OF AMERICA

10 9 8 7 6 5 4 3 2 1

This book is dedicated to

My wife, Nancy, and daughter, Rachael,
the very real loves of my life.

Bennie and Freda, who know the truth
because they are out there.

My agent Lori Perkins, who hustled this idea until it bled.

Barry at Berkley, who closed the deal.

And finally to this ultimate truth:
If I had not picked up the pen I would probably be playing
guitar in Kiss right now.

CONTENTS

acknowledgments

RESEARCHING THIS BOOK WAS LIKE WAKING UP AND finding myself in the middle of an *X-Files* episode. It went like this:

I attempted to contact Gillian Anderson through her management. Three calls and three messages produced nothing. Days after leaving the last message, I returned home to find a message from Anderson's manager on my answering machine. Just a name and number. I returned her call. She was out and would get back to me. Over the next two weeks I left a dozen more messages, but she didn't call back.

I tracked down Anderson's husband, Errol Clyde Klotz, at his place of work and left a message, then a second message a couple of days later. Klotz called back. I explained that I was writing a book about his wife, that it was not going to be a hatchet job, and requested an interview. He said he would have to think about it and that he would get back to me. Two hours later the telephone rang and an unidentified assistant to Klotz stated that his boss declined to be involved in the project.

Undaunted, I called the FBI in an attempt to get some comment about what the real bureau thought of Anderson's portrayal. An unnamed FBI official declined the request, saying oh-so-cryptically, "The *X-Files* people have their ducks in order."

Gordon Edelstein, Anderson's director in the play *The Philanthropist,* returned my call. He said he would be glad to talk to me but only after he called Gillian and received her permission. Well, I thought, that's that. He'll call back when pigs fly. A couple of days later, Edelstein called back and said, "Gillian said it was okay." I immediately looked skyward.

I continued to luck it. A director-writer on location in Scotland turned up just in time to offer his memories of working with Anderson on the documentary *Spies Above.* Another director rang up fresh from his vacation to say that he'd have to check with Anderson before talking about his dealings with the actress on the BBC series *Future Fantastic!* He called back a couple of days later to say that he had not been able to contact Anderson or her people but that he would talk anyway.

Other Deep Throats and Mr. Xs began to come out of the woodwork with their own pieces of the puzzle. Thanks to Ric Murphy, Lynne Meadows, Ronald Guttman, Tim Choate, Lou Puopolo, Fred Heimstra, Fred Dreher, Catherine Dreher, Scott Turkel, Mike Kuhn, Gavin Blair, Martha Ostertag, Kurt Sayenga, David McNab, John Khouri, and David Feldshuh.

And, of course, there was the long and winding paper trail that included *For Him Magazine, Dreamwatch, Sci-Fi Universe, Starlog, Starburst, Entertainment Weekly, TV Guide, Rolling Stone, People, US, Sydney Morning Herald, Sydney Sunday Telegraph, TV Week, Chicago Tribune, Cinefantastique, Detour, Movieline,* Canadian Broadcasting Corporation, *Houston Post, Los Angeles Times, New York Times, SFX, Hard Copy,*

McCall's, USA Today, Denver Post, Washington Times, TV Scene, Washington Post, Woman's Day, Sky International, and Associated Press.

Finally, to these writers whose word is law—James Swallow, Julianne Lee, Ian Spelling, Kyle Counts, Paula Vitaris, Deborah Starr Seibel, Joe Nazarro, Stephanie Mansfield, Kevin Stevens, Kathleen Toth, Gary Leigh, Steven Eramo, Simon Bacal, Richard Houldsworth, Bret Watson, David Bassom, Jane Killick, Tom Gilatto, Craig Tomashoff, Andrew Billen, Jon Matsumoto, Bronwen Gora, Michael Idato, Alex Strachan, Harriet Winslow, Jenny Cooney, James Glave, Andrew Denton, Alex Witchel, Sheryl Kahn, Lynn Elber, Matt Roush, Buzz McCain, Virginia Campbell, Lynne Melcombe, Allan Johnson, Anthony Noguera, David Hughes, and Daniel Nylander—let me know if I can return the favor.

introduction

GILLIAN ANDERSON: REALITY CHECK

THIS IS THE PLACE IN CELEBRITY BIOGRAPHIES where the author paints a picture of puffed-up, overwrought blather about how wonderful the subject of the tome is and why this person's career on the big screen or small tube is worthy of a critical, literary interpretation. But I'm not going to do that.

In fact, I'm not even going to state the obvious. I'm going to let Gordon Edelstein, who directed Gillian Anderson in the play *The Philanthropist* at a time when only a handful of theater aficionados had the slightest clue who Gillian Anderson was, do it for me. "I think it's funny and amazing that anybody should be writing a biography on somebody so young," he declared. "After all, she's just made one damned television show."

Edelstein is right on. Gillian Anderson is good, but she's not Hepburn (at least not yet). Most high school kids have a longer tardy list than Anderson has credits. But what Edelstein fails to recognize is the time-honored Hollywood equation: Ten percent talent and ninety percent luck equal stardom. Granted, Gillian Anderson's luck may have been pumped full of fortune and her talent squared. But Anderson would be the first to tell you that those two intangibles are what have made her and her alter ego, FBI skeptic Agent Dana Scully, the pinup goddess for the Internet generation.

The talent was obviously there in spades. And she was doing her best to play by the dues-paying rules. Acting in regional and off-Broadway plays, guest shots in forgettable TV episodes, a strong role in a little-seen film, and waitressing—lots of waitressing. So Gillian would have eventually bobbed to the surface, whether the conduit was *The X-Files, Sense and Sensibility, A Streetcar Named Desire,* or *Friday the 13th: Part X.* That she could act up a storm was never in question.

Luck is a whole different bag.

Do you know how many television pilots are created every year? Do you know how many pilots actually make it to series? Do you know how many series last longer than six episodes before the proverbial plug is pulled? How many shows even make it to a second season? Even fewer end up dotting the cultural landscape as pop culture icons. Yet when Gillian Anderson auditioned for and won the role on *The X-Files,* she began rolling the first of a long string of sevens.

The gods have chosen to give Gillian Anderson her shot, her moment in the sun, her foot in the door. That is the reason why this biography is being written. Gillian Anderson has been ordained the flavor of the moment. The next big thing. The blah, blah, blah.

If I'm wrong, Gillian Anderson will supernova when *The X-Files* ends and, ten years from now, she will be in science-fiction convention hell while this book will be gathering dust on some remainder table with a $1 price tag on it.

But if I'm right, and my gut tells me that I am, *The Anderson Files* will be the first of many career looks to come.

one

STAR BRIGHT . . . STAR FRIGHT

WHEN GILLIAN ANDERSON AND ERROL CLYDE Klotz were about to tie the knot in Hawaii in 1993, the star of the popular television series *The X-Files* recalls standing out in the open air, awaiting the words from the minister that would make the pair husband and wife, and looking up in the sky. "I don't know what I was looking for," Anderson reflects. "I don't think it was UFOs or anything like that. But I was definitely looking for something."

Perhaps a sign?

Gillian Anderson awoke early in the morning. She went to the window of her Melbourne, Australia, hotel room and drew back the curtains and looked out on a city that was slowly coming to life.

She should have seen the signs.

The sun, already up, was beating a hazy, black-spot reflection off the buildings. People walking on the sidewalks below seemed to be moving at half speed. Cars were moving at a crawl despite an absence of traffic. Melbourne was strangely muted amid the expected hustle and bustle of the day. Anderson rubbed the last bit of sleep from her eyes. She thought about room-service coffee. She thought about a shower. She thought about when the limo and the Australian PR types would be coming around.

But she immediately went to the crib where Piper, her daughter, had mercifully begun a regular pattern of sleeping through the night. Anderson looked in at the child, who was just beginning to stir. She smiled a calm, contented smile. Piper began to coo and opened her eyes. Anderson reached into the crib, picked up her daughter, put her to her shoulder, and began to slowly rock and sing softly to her.

After a few moments, Anderson rang up her nanny, who was situated in a room just down the hall. She was up and so Anderson, with Piper freshly diapered and with her first bottle of the day, walked down the hallway to the nanny's room. She kissed Piper goodbye and went back to her room. Anderson, secure in the knowledge that her child would be in safe hands for the course of her working day, was at peace.

And so she did not think about the signposts that the city of Melbourne was holding out for her that day.

Gillian Anderson should have seen Melbourne coming.

The clues, like any good *X-Files* story, were out there on just about every leg of her June 1996 promotional tour of Australia. The hint of something not quite right and very *X-Files*-like had manifested itself days before an estimated ten thousand fans turned up at a Brisbane mall.

Anderson was clearly unprepared for the mania that had followed her down under. Yes, she had seen the Australian fan mail and was alternately amused and appreciative of the support for herself and the show from this seemingly unrealized source. But with the acclaim, Anderson was quickly being reminded of the very thing she was still running from.

"When I think of fame, I think of the catch-22 nature of it," a clearly exhausted Anderson says to a Sydney reporter halfway through the trip. "I think of the benefit and the desire to be recognized for one's work and respected within the acting community, and that's about where the line has to be drawn for me."

Unfortunately for Anderson, the line on her sense of privacy and that of her family would come under constant attack in the twenty-four hours leading up to Brisbane.

When her limo pulled into the studios for the taping of a local program called *The Midday Show,* Anderson was only mildly surprised to find fans lining the road as she drove by. The surprise turned into legitimate concern for life and limb when, upon entering the studio proper, she looked to her rear and saw people climbing over the studio walls in an attempt to get close to her. The unbridled mania continued that night at a party thrown at the local branch of Planet Hollywood. Anderson was playing the game to the extent that she was letting a local photographer follow her around, literally recording her every move on film. But Anderson finally had enough, and when the photographer aimed his fish-eye lens in her direction yet another time, her look went cold and she put her hand up to the camera lens in that classic gesture of no more.

Anderson was definitely on the edge. At one point in this odyssey, she was asked by an inquiring mind why her daughter was not with her. Her response? "She is, we're just protecting her from you guys."

"Fame? It's like suffocation," states Anderson during a point in the Australian trip where exhaustion had taken on the persona of a constant companion. "I tend to be very private, so I don't get off on the paparazzi following me around or the intrusion aspect of it. I don't like big crowds. I'm in a rather vulnerable state of mind right now. I'm tending to run myself ragged, and so it can be incredibly intrusive and disorienting to place yourself in a situation where there are hundreds and thousands of people who want your attention. It gets emotionally draining."

Consequently, it was all those fears that were pushed to the limit in Brisbane. An estimated ten thousand fans, no doubt hearing of the mania that had been dogging their favorite actress, went from docile to rabid shortly after Anderson climbed the stage at the Brisbane mall and shouted a greeting to the sea of humanity. Anderson started out with a short thank you speech to the fans of Australia and then began signing a variety of things that were literally being thrust in her face.

Almost immediately, the rush was on. Fans surged toward the stage where Anderson was signing autographs and crushed and trampled many of those standing in front of the crowd. Anderson, that day, was surprised and concerned; she admonished the crowd by saying, "I really want to stay and sign more autographs but people are getting injured!" before cutting the appearance short. As she left Brisbane, Gillian Anderson was suddenly not quite right with the turn this trip to promote *The X-Files* was taking. Especially when a hookup with a New Zealand–based television interviewer was short-circuited, partially because of a technical screwup and, reading the look on Anderson's face, partially because of the interviewer's dogged determination to pry out of Anderson a confession about an off-screen romance between her and her costar David Duchovny.

"It's a rumor that was created out of thin air," says Anderson of this constant annoyance. "People automatically assume that because we work together that we're lovers as well. People just refuse to believe that we rarely see each other outside of our work and that we have very different lives."

Despite the pressure, Anderson took an emotional deep breath and pressed on.

Next stop, a mall in Sydney where twelve thousand screaming fans were ready to pounce. One person had spent the night sleeping in his car so he could be near the front of the stage when Gillian arrived. Those with slightly less determination began lining up at 5 A.M. for a 1:45 P.M. appearance. Word of mouth had spread like wildfire about the Beatlemania-like response to Anderson's appearances in the early part of the promotional tour and so it came as no surprise that no less than one hundred police officers and security officials were on hand when Anderson took the stage at 2 P.M.

"Hello! You guys look great!" screams Anderson. "Wow! This is fantastic!"

The crowd had been warned that any undue pushing or shoving would result in the immediate termination of the event, and initially the crowd was cooperative throughout Anderson's short thank you speech. But the minute a pen appeared in Anderson's hand, the crowd at the back began to lunge forward. Audible thuds could be heard as the screaming fans at the front hit the stage. People began to fall and were in immediate danger of being trampled and suffocated. Standby medical personnel waded into the crowd and began to pull the first of what would ultimately add up to eighty bodies from the throng. Anderson was immediately aware of what was going on and made some announcements to move back which were ignored. Finally, with a look that mirrored equal parts disappointment and amazement, Anderson left the stage.

What Gillian Anderson was seeing firsthand as her nondescript limo rolled through the streets of Melbourne, past good neighborhoods and not-so-good neighborhoods before pulling a sudden turn into the bowels of a Melbourne mall parking lot, was the raging, uncontrollable beast that was the dark side of stardom. And, looking out through the black, slightly frosted limo window into the equally black parking structure, the actress was well aware that the raging blind side of stardom could get even more strange. Kind of like an X-File.

Anderson emerges from the limo, her hazel eyes showing a mixture of exhaustion and excitement as she brushes absently at a lock of her conservatively cut hair. The actress, dressed in a dark pantsuit and wearing what has become her trademark wire-rimmed glasses, makes some small talk with her entourage.

At a signal a phalanx of muscular security types moves in and surrounds Anderson in a relaxed but formidable protective circle, making her already slight five-foot three-inch frame appear even smaller. The twenty-seven-year-old actress is ushered through a series of dimly lit hallways, her footfalls echoing slightly, that will lead to the center of the mall where Anderson is scheduled to meet, greet, and sign autographs for an estimated crowd of five thousand *X-Files* fans.

The actress has already faced bigger crowds on this, her first extensive solo promotional jaunt on behalf of her hit television series, but as she emerges into the center of the mall and looks out beyond the makeshift stage, her face reflects true amazement. The area in front of the stage is a sea of surging humanity, with cameras, *X-Files* videos, and photographs bobbing to the surface like so many whitecaps.

Amazed and, perhaps, a little bit uncertain.

Anderson looks around as she prepares to mount the steps in the back of the stage, wishing, perhaps, that her costar David Duchovny were part of her security team. "David is so much better at these things," Anderson says. But Mulder is nowhere to be seen, so Agent Scully must carry on alone.

A loud roar goes up as Anderson hits the stage. Flashbulbs go off. The crowd surges forward. The actress knows the drill by now. A brief greeting and then, felt-tip pen in hand, she reaches out to the sea of fans to receive and sign *X-Files* memorabilia. And, unfortunately, the crowd immediately begins to push toward the stage. There are immediate screams from the front of the crowd.

"Hey! We're getting crushed! Move back!"

A teenaged girl is shoved hard against the stage and crumples. A camera swinging wildly over the crowd strikes another in the head. A woman collapses, her hands clutching an *X-Files* video. Anderson, once again showing concern and no small amount of frustration, attempts to calm the crowd.

"People are getting squashed!" she yells out at the crowd. "We don't want to have to do any autopsies!"

But the crowd continues to slam forward, and, finally, as law enforcement and first-aid personnel wade into the throng and begin fishing the fallen fans out and dragging them to safety, Anderson sighs, says an only partially sincere thank you, and walks off the stage. Thankfully, no one was seriously injured during the Melbourne crush, but the price of sudden stardom was beginning to weigh heavily on the head of Gillian Anderson, who, during one moment of frustration during the Australian tour, was heard to exclaim, "What am I doing here!"

That was not the first time Gillian Anderson asked herself that question. The first time was most likely in January 1996 when the actress stood backstage in a makeshift greenroom at the Burbank Hilton hotel in Los Angeles. She was about to make her very first appearance at an *X-Files* fan convention. And the fact that she can hear roars of laughter coming from the convention hall, where another *X-Files* cast member, Dean Haglund (of infamous Lone Gunmen fame), has the gathered fans in stitches, is not making this maiden convention voyage any easier. Gillian glances uneasily at the fragments of a prepared speech in her hand. Her uneasy smile turns completely upside down. She is nervous. Very nervous. "I don't have anything funny to say," grouses Anderson as her entourage attempts to calm her fears. "What could I have been thinking?"

Costar David Duchovny has, to this point, been steadfast in refusing convention appearances and, through *The X-Files'* first two seasons, so had Anderson. But she acknowledges at her Los Angeles hotel a few days before the convention that she eventually decided to go public and meet her fans up close and personal. "I'm nervous about the whole thing. But it would be silly not to experience one. It will be my one and only convention experience."

Anderson is using this convention as a jumping-off point of sorts. After two years of essentially playing Agent Dana Scully as the logical second fiddle to that *X-Files* true believer Fox Mulder, the actress is attempting to boost to a higher level her public persona, which, until this point, has hinged largely on her getting pregnant and the hoops that unexpected blessed event caused the series' writers to jump through.

These days those self-same writers are having fewer headaches and more of a field day creating a new and much-improved special agent. They have already discovered that in Gillian Anderson they have a true diamond in the rough, an actress whose determination, intelligence, and boundless energy would make keeping Scully in the background as a one-note, logical thinker a true crime against nature.

Consequently, as *The X-Files* in its second season progressed from cult hit to critical and ratings top dog and graduated to a full-blown *Star Trek*–level pop culture phenom well into its third season, Scully, in Anderson's capable hands, has leveled the show's playing field. Gone, to a large extent, is her constant and somewhat one-dimensional doubting Thomas persona. In its place is a character who now regularly goes out on a limb in the name of Mulder's whacked-out theories while still maintaining an enticing, hard-to-convince, logical side. And though romance between the two characters has long since been given up for dead by everybody connected with the show, Scully is now being allowed moments of real playfulness and banter with Mulder that regularly heat and lighten up the show's normally somber, paranormal proceedings.

"Personally I think Scully has been chasing in Mulder's footsteps long enough," offered Anderson in a 1995 conversation. "The writers have certainly written her as being competent enough to do the investigations, and it's getting tiring to always be one step behind. At first it made sense, but now I think everybody has decided to move forward with her."

And Anderson is proving more than equal to the task of dealing with a character that is growing by leaps and bounds. "She's very smart," says *X-Files* writer Glen Morgan. "The writers have thrown her some real curves and she's been able to handle them all."

X-Files creator Chris Carter has also been impressed by the actress's work ethic. "Gillian is very hardworking, and given the long hours we put in on this show, I can't remember the last time I heard a complaint out of her. She was at work each day right up until two days before the birth of her daughter. That says a lot."

Also saying a lot in a backdoor sort of way is Gillian's costar David Duchovny, who chuckles, "She's the best Scully I've ever worked with."

And in the inevitable merchandising rush in the wake of *The X-Files'* unprecedented success, Gillian has seen her face and form end up in some conventional and unconventional places. She is featured monthly on the cover of a mainstream comic-book adaptation of the series. For the fringies, Penthouse Comix's X-rated line offered an unauthorized one-shot story line in which Anderson does the nasty in a spoof of the show. Throw in the T-shirts, posters, original novels, magazine covers, and coffee mugs, and fans have found all the building blocks necessary to construct a literal shrine to the actress.

A lot less fathomable to Anderson in the wake of her growing popularity are the accolades that come her way via the Internet and any number of chat groups and computer forums that sprang up along the superhighway even before *The X-Files* wrapped its first season.

For the novices, there is the Gillian Anderson FAQ (frequently asked questions) web site, which is a just-the-facts link to the actress's birthdate, education, phonetic pronunciation of her name (Jill-ee-un), height, hair color, and so forth. For the more esoteric, there's the Gillian Anderson Sounds Page, which faithfully offers sound snippets of classic Scully dialogue. Male worshipers sign on to the Gillian Anderson Testosterone Brigade, where they regularly pay homage to her beauty and sometimes her brains. Female fans pay tribute to her brains on the Gillian Anderson Estrogen Brigade and the Gillian Anderson Neuro-Transmitter Association. And it is in such computer meeting places (a phenomenon that has elicited from Anderson the response "It just tickles me") that the truth behind what makes Dana Scully and Gillian Anderson the subject of such adoration flickers daily across highlighted computer bulletin boards.

"Ms. Anderson is, for us, the personification of the real woman," read one Testosterone Brigade missive. "Gillian Anderson is not a sexless brainiac," stated a recent NeuroTransmitter message. "She couldn't be." And then there's a bit of understatement, once again courtesy of the boys in the Testosterone band. "She is not yet another bimbo chasing criminals in high heels."

It is in this last statement that we get the bottom-line truth of why Gillian, aka Dana, has become so popular so fast. In a world populated by aliens, monsters, and a shadowy, suspect government, Dana Scully is a real cool customer. With the emphasis on real.

She does nothing without a logical reason and won't do anything out of character simply to advance a story along or prop up a sagging script. There's a reason why she has not slept with Mulder. There's also a reason why she shot Mulder in one particularly harrowing *X-Files* outing. Dana Scully was being true to character rather than to the cliché conventions of television.

And it is those very TV clichés that have made Anderson, by contrast, the pinup girl for the smart generation. In a television landscape littered with brainless blow-up *Baywatch* dolls and cold, one-dimensional *Star Trek* automatons, Gillian Anderson, attractive in a not-quite-classic way and capable of subtle twists and emotional turns, is an enticing bit of envelope pushing. A thinking man's crumpet, according to her most lustful fans. In other words, Scully and Anderson, and let's face it, the two are emotionally and attitudinally joined at the hip, are that giant step forward in characterization that breaks new ground constantly and always keeps audiences guessing and, most important, wanting more.

"Scully is a great part," proclaims Anderson very early in the production of the first season of *The X-Files*. "She's strong, she's independent, and she's very smart. Scully is a very appealing woman's role. I think that men and women are equally attracted to Scully because of her honesty, intelligence, and passion about her work. Those are qualities that both sexes can appreciate."

X-Files creator Chris Carter, who stacked the future of the show by insisting that Anderson, rather than a cookie-cutter Hollywood bimbo, play Scully, also realized early on that Anderson and Scully was a hand-to-glove fit. "Gillian's smart and she's ambitious, which is what her character is. She has to compete with the guys and still maintain a sense of her own femininity both in life and in terms of her character."

Bottom line, a marriage mixing imagination and talent has combined to make Gillian Anderson, who just over three years ago was an unknown with a string of East Coast theater appearances, the lead in a little-seen film, a voiceover for an audiobook, and a guest shot on a short-lived dramatic TV series to her credit, a 1990s pop, dare we say it, Gen X icon, dancing on the brink of stardom. And stardom, acknowledges the actress, is something that's taking a bit of getting used to, her perceptions of which have literally changed with the seasons.

Interviewed shortly after *The X-Files* premiered, when she was single, childless, and largely naive to the ways of impending stardom, Anderson offered, "If I thought about it [stardom] too much, it would probably scare the hell out of me. Right now I'm just taking it as it comes. I guess it's a pretty big deal." By 1995, though, Anderson, now married to production designer Errol Clyde Klotz and the mother of an eighteen-month-old daughter named Piper, had changed her tune. "I've gotten much more protective of myself and my boundaries. I can't go places without people recognizing me. Sometimes it makes me want to hide."

Back at the *X-Files* convention, hiding is definitely on Gillian Anderson's immediate agenda as Dean Haglund goes off to thunderous applause. Gillian is still nervous, but as the hall's lights dim and a montage of Scully-related bits begins to flash on a giant screen to whoops, hollers, and applause, the fear seems to melt away as she laughs at this example of what one character in one television series has brought her.

Anderson shrugs and rolls her eyes in a

"here goes nothing" gesture and strides onto the stage. At first sight of her the audience, already primed to a fever pitch, goes crazy. The applause and screaming reach the level of a jet engine. Young children and teenagers, holding bouquets of flowers, rush to the stage and deposit their offerings on the stage. Gillian is standing at the center of the stage, clearly overwhelmed. All thoughts of giving a formal speech are immediately put aside as she stands, soaking up the accolades. Finally the response subsides, and Anderson, still in a state of happy shock, approaches the microphone. The signs have been there all along. Gillian Anderson finally sees them.

"Does anybody have any questions?"

two

MY PARENTS WERE CIRCUS GEEKS

THE WINDS OF CHANGE WERE BLOWING THROUGH the world during the month of August 1968. Soviet tanks were lining the border of Czechoslovakia, preparing to rattle into the streets of Prague to squash an experiment in freedom and self-determination that had grown tiresome. In India, a week of flooding had brought the death toll to one thousand.

And in Chicago, things were starting to heat up. Caravans of antiwar protesters were arriving by the busload and carload, their counterculture attire and attitude presenting an odd, almost Fellini-esque contrast to the all-American vibe and red, white, and blue bunting that was going up in preparation for the Democratic National Convention, which, in a matter of days, would nominate Hubert Humphrey as the party's presidential candidate to do battle with Richard Nixon in the fall.

Outside the convention center, cops would beat the protesters, and the world would never be the same. Within shouting distance of the Democratic National Convention and the battleground that would be fought for and lost in Grant Park, lesser news was also being made: Gillian Anderson was born on August 9, 1968, in Chicago, Illinois.

The first child born to Edward and Rosemary Anderson, working-class parents who were attempting, in a late-1960s climate of extreme freedom and possibilities, to find their career and life choices. When she was two years old, Gillian's parents, whom she later jokingly described as "circus geeks" in response to the question of what they did for a living, uprooted the family and traveled to Puerto Rico.

Puerto Rico, which the Andersons concede was little more than a lifestyle find-yourself stopover, lasted barely a year before they, with a sudden sense of purpose and goal, immigrated to England, where Edward Anderson, in January 1971, registered at the London Film School with an eye toward furthering his goal of entering film production work.

During that period, the Anderson family jumped from the middle-class residence at Clapton Common to the more up-market neighborhood of 19 Rosebury Gardens. Edward Anderson completed the two-year course in 1972 and, according to school records, graduated with an excellent rating. The family elected to stay in London, where he pursued film production work.

Gillian attended the local middle-class Coleridge Primary School during much of the 1970s, developing a decided accent, a sophistication far beyond her years, and a strong inclination toward science fact and the paranormal.

Anderson recalls that at a rather early age her interest in science in general and in a career in biology in particular manifested itself in regular trips to the backyard to dig up earthworms. She was barely old enough to read when *Omni* magazine, in particular the section devoted to UFOs, began to top her reading list.

The actress's recollection of her childhood years is couched in fragments of memories. "I would have to say my childhood years were fairly normal. I knew my father was doing the type of work not many people were doing. My parents were always fairly liberal so I guess I was given a certain degree of freedom that a lot of children did not have. And I guess you could say I was a bit of a tomboy, getting into things that the boys would do."

Anderson's school years at Coleridge were marked by good grades, a constant circle of friends, and even at that early age, a high degree of both confidence and childish arrogance. Reporter Lowri Turner's (a correspondent for the *London Sunday Mirror*) recent investigation into the actress's childhood years paints a less-than-pretty picture of a girl who, she reports, was already a bit of a wild child. "I interviewed a number of her former classmates, and according to them, she was the kid from hell. They claimed she was a bully and that she would regularly send notes to kids saying, 'I'll get you when the school bell rings.'"

Anderson, with an eye toward the obscure in her life, remembers that the first boy she ever kissed was an English lad named Adam. She also laughingly recalls that her London years introduced her to profanity and the first knowledge of sex. "I was very much into swearing as a child. I remember asking my mother what 'fuck' meant, what fucking was, and to this day, I can't remember on my life what her response was. I remember hearing that word for the first time when I was eight on the school playground from a kid who was twelve. . . . He fancied me and I fancied him, but I was scared to death because his affection was like grown-up affection. He may have even done the fuck word. And I had no idea what it meant."

The family stayed in London until 1979, when the Anderson clan decided to return to America. They settled in Grand Rapids, Michigan, where Edward and Rosemary Anderson settled in to establish an American upbringing for their daughter and to start anew their careers in film post-production and computer analysis. Grand Rapids was also where a now thoroughly

British-minded Gillian would attend her first day of school on American soil.

For the American-born Anderson, her first day in America in more than 10 years was an immediate, traumatic experience. "There was a certain feeling of displacement," she concedes. "Moving into a small town after growing up in London gave me a feeling of total powerlessness."

three

SHE'S A REBEL

Gillian Anderson graduated in the class of 1986 from City High School in Grand Rapids, Michigan. As her yearbook picture will attest, she was very much the rebel with punked-out hair, clothes off a secondhand-store rack, and, most telling, a look that said defiant with a capital D. And the actress recalls that the caption underneath it indicated that her future would not be on the right side of the law. "I was voted class clown and most likely to be arrested," she laughs.

But visions of Gillian behind bars were definitely not in the picture the first day a then-eleven-year-old Anderson strode confidently onto the school yard of Fountain Elementary School to begin the 1979 school year. It was the classic case of first-day jitters. Anderson's parents dropped her off in front of the school. She was nervous. But with the assurance from her parents that everything was going to be all right, she stepped out of the car and walked across campus. She readily admits she was uncomfortable, a big part of her homesick for London, the only real home she had known. When the school bell rang, however, Anderson, hiding her insecurities, strode confidently into her classroom.

Fred Heimstra, her fifth-grade teacher at Fountain, recalls that Gillian Anderson, during her first year back in the United States was nothing if not normal. "She was a well-rounded, normal kid," relates the teacher. "Gillian was very outgoing and had quite a few friends." Heimstra, who offers that Gillian "was an above-average student" who "excelled in language arts and literature" and who "really had an interest in drama and the arts even at that early age," also remembers a sense of sophistication about the young girl that he feels was part and parcel of her British upbringing. "Gillian was very sophisticated, far beyond her years," says Heimstra. "It was obvious when you talked to her and when she did her reports and other schoolwork. It was very plain that she knew a few more things about the world than the kids who had spent their entire lives in Grand Rapids. . . . She was not withdrawn by any stretch of the imagination," he continues, "and there was this seeming heightened sense of sensitivity about her. She was very in tune with the atmosphere in the classroom and the situations that were going on around her."

Anderson's memory of those early school days is a lot different. "Being in Grand Rapids was different. It was pretty normal and it was pretty strange. In a sense it was good for me because I got my kicks." But she also recalls incidents of "being made fun of because of my accent" and being "bullied by my classmates." "I was withdrawn and unpopular," she says. "I was always off in my own little world or being sent to the principal's office for talking back."

Around this time Gillian's parents decided to expand the family and had two more children, a son, Aaron, and a second daughter, Zoe, in rather rapid succession. The sudden addition of siblings into what had been a solo existence further alienated Anderson from the normal conventions of family life and sent her scurrying into the waiting arms of the burgeoning Grand Rapids punk rock scene. "I went back to London for the summer when I was twelve and I was suddenly taken with the whole punk thing," remembers Anderson. "I returned to the States with a stud in my nose. It was hilarious. I would walk sideways around my dad so he wouldn't see it."

Gillian embraced the harsh sounds of bands like The Circle Jerks and The Dead Kennedys. She shaved her head into a three-foot purple Mohawk, put a ring through her nose, began wearing junk-store black clothing and started her journey into adolescence as the poster child for what many perceived as the doomed generation. "I used to be a good little girl in corduroys. All of a sudden I put red dye in my hair, started to wear funky miniskirts, and gradually progressed to more outrageous outfits."

And into a downward academic and personal spiral. "By the time I got to junior high school my grades were real bad," she recalls. "I was daydreaming, pulling pranks. I was in the principal's office every other day. I suppose it wasn't anything you would consider high-crime kinds of things. It would be for things like talking, putting shaving cream in lockers, stealing papers, and throwing paper airplanes. I was getting my kicks, but I was also very confused and a loner."

Anderson soon found herself among kindred spirits who would practice the punk ethic, an anti-establishment lifestyle based around the high-energy, up-yours attitude of the emerging punk rock music scene. Normally shy and reticent to jump into new situations, Anderson was quick to join in the small but loud group of Grand Rapids punks hell-bent on upholding the traditions started by their founding fathers in London. "We would walk down the street and give the finger to whoever stared at us," recalled Anderson with more than a hint of amusement in a 1996 conversation. "We'd go hear bands, smash against each other, and jump off the stage. At that time it was definitely cool to get hurt."

Anderson's desire to hurt began to manifest itself in various ways. She began to drink at a very early age and had more than a nodding acquaintance with drugs. In the midst of this emotional roller-coaster ride, Gillian, in 1981 at the age of thirteen, lost her virginity to one of her punk rock associates. Even in a 1996 conversation, Anderson's discomfort with that memory was apparent. She does not acknowledge the boy's name and only hints that he was just a punk guy who grew up extreme. But she is straightforward in her memory of her first sexual experience not being pleasant. "It was awkward, stupid, unadulterated crap. It was not incredibly romantic, and it was not the best lay I ever had. How could it be at thirteen?"

A year later Anderson entered City High School with, given the circumstances, a decent grade point average and more than a passing interest in marine biology as a career choice. Catherine Dreher, a student at City High when Anderson was there, remembers the first time she saw Anderson walking down the hallway toward her. "She was a little intimidating. She gave off this attitude of being totally self-confident.

It was like you couldn't touch her and you couldn't hurt her. She was one tough girl."

Another former classmate at City High, who requests anonymity, remembers Gillian Anderson as being "a cross between Madonna and Johnny Rotten." "She had style and a lot of presence," the mystery voice continues. "She was only five three, but I certainly would not have wanted to pick a fight with her. Since she had lived in London for several years, she had an English accent that gave her an authentic punk edge. Gillian had attitude for days. She was outspoken, rebellious, and didn't seem to care what others thought of her."

Anderson, despite a painful first sexual experience, continued to court and couple on a fairly regular basis during her high school years. The trend toward much older men also continued, as did the tendency for sex to be less than romantic. Gillian, at age fourteen, had her first serious relationship, with a twenty-four-year-old punk rocker. When not drifting in and out of her parents' home, Gillian and her lover would often find themselves crashing in warehouses or on a friend's apartment floor. "He was in a punk band," Anderson remembers of her older lover. “I used to sneak cans of food out of our house to give to him and buy him soft drinks and cigarettes from the local stores.”

Outwardly Anderson was still defiant, embracing the excesses of life and, more often than not, looking for a fight rather than a friend. However, looking back on that pivotal relationship in a 1996 interview, the actress recalled, rather painfully, how she felt it was part and parcel of the fact that she was on the wrong track. “I guess I felt comfortable in that relationship because I felt dirty, grungy, and angry. I really did not like myself too much at that point.”

Anderson’s self-loathing manifested itself in extreme physical and emotional swings. She was at times noticeably overweight. She would also go to the other extreme and was often viewed as acutely thin and unhealthy looking. “I don’t want to go into that,” said Anderson recently when a reporter asked her if she had been bulimic as a youth.

Anderson, who hung with what she describes as “a very atheist crowd,” continued to wear black as her prevailing color scheme, and it proved to be a mirror of her soul at that point, a soul that was quite often introverted and seemingly forever in hiding from real and imaginary monsters. And the way Anderson remembers it, her unorthodox appearance and demeanor was, at that time, a way of feeling in control. "I never really felt attractive for years," she related in a 1996 interview, "and it was only when I started to shave my head and dressed differently that I realized I had a voice in who I was and what I stood for. It was an angry phase that I was going through, and it served me well at the time. I think it made me a much more independent and strong person. I dressed in black, wore combat boots, and had hair that stood up six feet tall, but still people were attracted to me. So it worked. But, at times, I knew what I was doing was also a crutch."

Gillian Anderson seemed headed for a mighty big fall when, during what many would consider the bleakest moments of her high school years, she happened upon acting. To this day, Anderson has not put into words what about acting, especially on a high school level, attracted her. However, she has a clear picture of immediately embracing it. "I think acting, to a large extent, saved me," Anderson recalls. "It gave me an outlet to express myself."

The extent of Anderson's participation in City High's dramatic program is sketchy at best. What is known for a fact is that as a senior she appeared in the small role of Police Officer No. 2 in the school's production of *Arsenic and Old Lace.* Her high school credits also included the starring role in the production of *The Zoo Story,* a tale of human emotion in control and out of control. And, according to former student Catherine Dreher, Anderson's acting skills, even at that early juncture, were immediately evident. "She played this totally insane character and I was totally floored by her performance. Watching her on stage I was seeing a whole different person. Gillian had this incredible talent."

Encouraged by this newfound passion, Anderson, as part of her school's senior-year internship program, went to work at the nearby Grand Rapids Civic Theater. Paul Dreher, who heads up the Civic, laughs as he recalls the day the then-seventeen-year-old Gillian Anderson came in and interviewed for the job. "When I first met her, I thought she was kind of a mess," he chuckles at the memory. "Gillian was in a real punk phase, and the way she was dressed was pretty outlandish. She had this ugly dyed red hair, heavy huge black lines around her eyes, black lipstick, a ring in her nose, and this ever-present hideous black shift that she wore. She seemed a bit standoffish, and I got the distinct impression that she didn't like me too much."

Anderson worked in the front office for a year, answering telephones and doing basic receptionist duties. By all accounts she was a good worker, and, although she chaffed at having to do things like answer telephones, she was always at her station on time. Dreher recalls that his assistant manager was constantly on her case about her appearance. "But it didn't seem to have any effect." Dreher remembers, too, that Gillian was intent on getting out from behind the desk and out on the stage. "All she wanted to do was act and she seemed bound and determined to do it."

Anderson states in several interviews that she auditioned for and won a role in a production at the Civic Theater but does not recall the play. "I got the part and then

I felt extremely happy," she reported in an early 1990s interview. "I felt like I had found my place."

Dreher concurs that Anderson, during her internship, actually did audition for him for the role of Emily in the Civic's production of *Our Town.* But, he recalls quite different results. "Gillian probably would have been pretty good in the role, but she insisted on auditioning in the same clothes that she always wore. Needless to say her audition did not go down real well. I don't remember actually saying anything to her at the time but I know I thought, 'Girl, if you want to act, you'd better put on a little bit of the persona you're trying to portray.' She did not get the part, and she probably never forgave me. I know she seemed real upset at the time. And I know she never auditioned for me again."

Mike Kuhn used to cross paths with Gillian Anderson on an infrequent basis. His new wave band Swampuggi would occasionally play with Anderson's boyfriend's band, White Room. He recalls the Grand Rapids scene at that time as "pretty small and pretty tame." He also recalls Anderson, at that point, as being "about as wild as anybody was at age seventeen." But when, as a college senior, in 1985, he was in need of some actors for his film school project, he also discovered something else about Anderson.

"I didn't know that much about her at the time except from the few times I had seen her at shows," remembers Kuhn. "But I had heard through friends that she had (allegedly) acted in community theater. . . . So I met with her, gave her the script; she read it and said 'sure.'"

The filmmaker's first impression of Anderson was positive. "She seemed to be very wise for her age. Gillian seemed to have a good worldview and a good understanding of things. She was very intelligent and had a certain spunkiness to her that just blew me away."

Kuhn's film, entitled *Three at Once,* was, by the filmmaker's own description, "an artsy fartsy thing" in which three actors emote on their hopes and fears as they descend on a party. Very much a talking (with the exception of a game of charades) piece, this eight-minute black-and-white film was shot over a three-day period in the fall of 1985 in a restaurant/office complex called The Castle. "Admittedly, the concept of the film was kind of obscure but, as we were filming, I discovered that [Gillian] had a real grasp of where I was coming from with the piece and she was able to flesh out what was a very one-dimensional character."

Three at Once was shown at a local Grand Rapids festival in 1986 and resurfaced again in a Seattle festival in 1996. Kuhn recalls that "The first time Gillian saw the film, the first comment out of her mouth was that I had spelled her sister's name [who had worked behind the scenes on the film] wrong. Beyond that she really didn't say anything."

Anderson finished out her senior year in fine punk style, continuing to drink and to raise hell. Her grades, surprisingly, remained average and were good enough for her to graduate. But on the night she received her diploma . . .

"Gillian! The cops are coming! Let's get out of here!"

Anderson relates that "after a night of total excess," she and her fellow revelers broke back into the high school and were about to vandalize everything in sight as a going-away gift when the local police showed up and caught them in the act. "It was awful. I was arrested and thrown in jail. I had to call my boyfriend to come and bail me out. But I ended up spending several hours in jail before he came and got me."

Anderson's boyfriend, who had been with her earlier in the evening but who went home when things started getting really wild, took a while to get up the bail money. When he finally arrived at the jail, the first thing he saw was Anderson staring out from behind the bars. "It was a punk stage I went through," she later recalled.

Where Anderson would end up following graduation from City High was anybody's guess. More than one local echoed her high school yearbook prediction and figured drugs, teenage motherhood, and an early grave would be her epitaph. But despite the continued rough edges, others saw a determination, most likely brought on by her interest in acting, that would somehow see her through. So it came as little surprise when Anderson proudly announced that she had applied to the prestigious Goodman Theater School for the coming fall semester.

Ric Murphy walked into the auditorium of the Goodman Theater School on the campus of Chicago's famed De Paul University. It was midmorning, slightly overcast. It was time for the annual late-summer rite of passage for the school's professor of acting, which was to wade through the latest batch of an estimated eight hundred auditions to round out a class for the next four-year cycle, which would begin the fall 1986 semester.

The early part of the auditions went pretty much as Murphy anticipated. Young men and women, in varying degrees of informal dress, reading selected passages from famous and obscure works. Murphy is a practiced hand, making quick notations in a notebook and his own mental decision within thirty seconds of the beginning of the reading. At one point Murphy looked at his list of prospective students.

"Gillian Anderson."

Anderson got up from her seat. Murphy's jaw dropped.

"She was dressed in this outrageously loud aquamarine jumpsuit," laughingly recalls Murphy. "I just stared and stared. I didn't have a clue as to what was going on with this woman."

Per the requirements of the course, Gillian opened the pages of the first of her two required audition pieces and began to read. There was a sense of tension and suspense as Anderson went through her lines in a manner that was equal parts normal conversation and over-the-top emoting. It was a sensation that was not lost on Murphy, who was frantically scribbling in his notebook. "There was a breathless sort of energy to her that was immediate and quite stunning," recalls the instructor. "She displayed an immediate presence and a real sense of anticipation. I felt I was about to discover something new and different about her as I was watching her read."

Gillian Anderson had made the grade. But though the Mohawk, the nose ring, and some of the other vestiges of her raging youth had been left behind, Anderson, through much of her college career, would continue to battle a variety of personal demons.

She remained very introverted away from the theater environment and, though a bit more particular in her liaisons, Gillian, in a 1996 conversation, was forthcoming in stating that through her college years she remained "somewhat promiscuous." She confided, "I think I felt that if somebody liked me, then I was supposed to sleep with them. I didn't realize, at that point, that I had a choice in the matter. I don't think I enjoyed sex much back then."

Anderson, in that same conversation, was obviously uncomfortable in discussing another of her college-years vices—alcohol. "I loved alcohol," she sighed. "I actually liked alcohol a bit too much. Drinking made me feel much stronger, more confident, and sexier."

Acting ultimately turned out to be the light at the end of this dismal tunnel. Her outlook, while still occasionally dampened by doubt and depression, began to change for the better. Her grades improved dramatically.

"It was like acting freed me up," she reflects. "It gave me an outlet for a lot of crap I was carrying around."

Anderson's first two years at the Goodman were taken up primarily with the techniques of improvisation and scene study. And, in those areas, Murphy recalls, Gillian excelled. "In that first year of instruction, I discovered that she had a real capacity for surprise. You always felt that you were trafficking in the unknown when Gillian got up to do an exercise. Her powers of observation were real intense. I remember that, during our first year, the class had an assignment to go out and observe somebody and then come into class and do that person. Gillian went out and observed a waitress. When she came in and started to imitate her I could tell that she had really put a lot into it, right down to the way she moved and handled things. It was really amazing. I knew early on that, in Gillian, I had this electric personality on my hands." A personality that was finally allowed to take center stage in her junior year at Goodman in a variety of productions that tested her dramatic and comedic skills. Anderson appeared in productions of *A Flea in Her Ear, Serious Money, Last Summer at Bluefish Cove, Romeo and Juliet,* and *In a Northern Landscape.* "There was a power in her work," reflects Murphy. "She was a real presence in *Serious Money* and *Last Summer in Bluefish Cove.* And you had to be there to see how wonderful her comic timing could be in *A Flea in Her Ear*. In that play she played the maid, which was, in its inception, a very tiny part. But she took the part and made it an eccentric, odd, and extremely strange starring role."

Anderson, during the first season of *The X-Files,* agreed with Murphy's assessment. "Up to that point the things I had been doing were pretty serious stuff. So *A Flea in Her Ear* was good for me because it allowed me to explore the comedic side of acting."

But despite raves in the local press and constant encouragement from Murphy and other faculty members, the actress's lingering doubts about herself and her ability were never too far from her thoughts. "She never thought she was going to be able to make a living as an actress," recalls Murphy, "and it became more acute the closer she came to graduation. "It was never a question for me. But it was definitely a question for her. Gillian had some pretty strong doubts about herself."

But kitchens were tough to come by, so in a creative burst Davis switched gears.

The filmmaker, whose previous experimental movies relied heavily on a pro-feminist stance, was well aware that abortion was very much the hot-button topic during the 1988 election year. And so *A Matter of Choice* was born in the filmmaker's mind. *A Matter of Choice*, which was designed as a five-minute, black-and-white, silent one-character study, begins with a long shot of a woman about to enter an alley. The woman in question is arriving for her appointment to have an abortion. She walks up to a door with a coat hanger logo on it, looks at her watch, and sees that she is five minutes early. The remainder of the film is various shots of the woman pacing and close-ups of her face. At the end of *A Matter of Choice,* the woman goes through the door. Davis, whose filmmaking style was more conceptual than scripted at that point, knew casting this project would be difficult.

He needed somebody who could convey emotions through facial expressions and gestures without being too over-the-top. Davis was perplexed. He could not think of anybody in his circle of acting choices who was capable of pulling it off. Then he thought of Anderson, the only woman his instincts told him he could trust to make *A Matter of Choice* work.

Davis made this decision not too far from the Wabash Avenue alley he had chosen to shoot the film. It was midmorning when he called Anderson. He wanted to know if she was available that afternoon and could she meet him downtown in an hour. Anderson said she would be there. When Anderson arrived at the alley, she found a cameraman and Davis standing at the entrance. The look on her face was equal parts amusement and curiosity. She did not have a clue what would be required of her. Davis briefly explained what *A Matter of Choice* was about. He was half expecting a barrage of questions regarding motivation and the like, but Anderson had listened intently, and when Davis finished, she said she needed a moment. Thirty seconds later she told Davis she was ready.

A Matter of Choice was completed in two hours, and a big reason for that was Anderson's ability to give Davis exactly what he wanted. Davis was so swept off his feet by the dimension of her performance that during a pause to change camera setups he asked Anderson if she had done a lot of films. Anderson responded that it was the first time she had ever been in front of a camera. Davis, dumbfounded, responded by saying that she was pretty good.

Anderson saw the completed *A Matter of Choice* a week later and by all accounts was pleased with it. Those around her felt the subject matter was never of any overriding concern to her but that the quality of the work was.

It was in 1989, a year before Anderson graduated, that the first of many intriguing rumors regarding the still very amateur actress began circulating. That was the year that Anderson, reportedly, did her first film, a small part in a movie for television called *Home Fires Burning*. For the record: Not true.

The rumor, most likely, had its roots in a 1992 review in a New York magazine that, for whatever reason, mistakenly headlined a review of the film that Anderson was in, called *The Turning*, as *Home Fires Burning*. Subsequently, this credit has been wrongly attributed to Anderson in more than one biography. Setting the record straight is the director of *Home Fires Burning,* Glenn Jordan, who insists that Anderson, to his memory, was not in his film. The director even went so far as to dig out an old cast list and could not find Anderson's name anywhere, not even as an extra.

Shortly before she graduated from De Paul (with a bachelor of fine arts degree), Anderson's confidence seemed to soar. Having topflight representation like the William Morris Agency probably helped. But those who saw her around campus those last couple of months could tell. Anderson had overcome a very big hurdle in her personal and professional life. She felt in control of her own destiny and confident in her ability to make a living as an actress.

Consequently, Anderson was quick to jump at her agent's insistence that she, at 11 P.M. on a predetermined night, pack her Volkswagen Rabbit so full "that I could not see out the rearview mirror" and set out for New York City. "I had it in my mind that I should leave on a certain day," she recalls with an aside to her growing belief in karma, “but it took longer to pack than I expected. I drove for a while and then pulled off the side of the road to take a nap. The car was so full that I had to crouch up in a fetal position.”

four

BITING THE BIG APPLE

IT'S NEVER TOO FAR FROM COLD IN NEW YORK CITY.

Even when the snow has taken its leave, you can always count on a stiff breeze or an unexpected shower to bring temperatures and temperaments to the basement. But this was a crazy-quilt kind of midmorning. The sun was just now peaking through a thick patch of clouds. Coats were coming off and rolled-up sleeves exposed to the surprising warmth; a seemingly appropriate welcome for Gillian Anderson as her car pulled to the curb in front of an apartment building in a funky part of New York's Greenwich Village. Spread across her front seat was a newspaper open to the

"For Rent" page. Several possibilities were circled. A couple had already been X'd out. Her backseat was piled to near overflowing with belongings. Gillian looked around, finally got out of her car, and walked up a flight of stairs. Minutes later she was back down on the street.

It was not much. But Gillian Anderson, newly arrived in the Big Apple, was finally home. "I loved New York," she remembers of her first days in the Big Apple. "I swore I'd never leave."

Anderson wasted little time settling into the lifestyle of the struggling actress. She went on lots of auditions for primarily off-off-Broadway and experimental, fringe productions and failed to get a part. When she had any money left, which was rare after paying the rent, Gillian would go to the theater and would inevitably end up in the last row of the balcony, "getting nosebleeds and looking down at these unidentifiable specks on the stage."

To pay the rent, Anderson settled quickly into that traditional dues-paying job, waitressing. Her first waitressing job; lost in the mists of memory, came and went without a record. Her second and last dues-paying job, however, did leave its mark. "I knew she was fairly new in town and I knew she was an actress," recalls Dojo restaurant manager Scott Turkel of his initial meeting with Anderson in 1990. "She didn't appear to be too naive or vulnerable. I got the immediate impression that she really knew what she was doing."

Turkel, who claims for the record that Anderson, during her four-month stay at the restaurant, "was a pretty good waitress," relates that Anderson by that time had dropped her punk look. "She was fairly normal looking by Village standards and, based on what I've heard about her over the years, had pretty much toned things down. All I can figure was that she had either stopped the punk thing on her own or did it to get the job."

Anderson was at Dojo's long enough for the manager to get a fairly clear picture of her. "She was friendly but she could be feisty. I remember one day at work I said something she didn't like and she kicked me right in the leg. I went out with her one night after work and had a drink with her and we talked, and I remember her being very serious and focused about what she wanted to do."

Because what she wanted to do was act, Turkel was not too surprised when "she walked into the restaurant one day and said 'I'm out of here.' It happens all the time. I just figured she had gotten an acting job somewhere."

Anderson, in point of fact, had not so much gotten an acting job as she had stumbled into one of those lucky Hollywood-style breaks.

The Manhattan Theater Company, one of the most prestigious houses on the Great White Way, was well into the rehearsals for the play *Absent Friends,* the Alan Ayckbourn tragicomedy about dysfunctional friends and questionable sexual politics. Mary Louise Parker had already auditioned for and captured the role of the ill-natured Evelyn, and the company was well into its first week of rehearsals when it experienced a major setback.

"Mary Louise had to drop out because of a conflicting job," relates *Absent Friends* director Lynne Meadow of the actress's decision to leave the production to appear in the movie *Grand Canyon*. "We were in rehearsal already and we were very desperate to find someone. It was a very odd situation." A situation that Anderson's agents at William Morris sought to take advantage of.

Gillian went in to read the role of Evelyn, and director Meadow recalls being pleasantly surprised. "Gillian had never done a play before in New York. All I knew about her was that she had just finished acting school in Chicago. She came to the audition a complete unknown. Nobody had ever seen her before. But she did the audition and I thought she was fantastic. She was perfect for the role of Evelyn. But we called her back for a second reading just to make sure it had not been a fluke. And when the second reading turned out to be every bit as good as the first, we took the leap and hired somebody who was completely unknown and totally inexperienced."

Nobody was more aware of the risk the *Absent Friends* production was taking than Anderson, who, at this late date, was still carrying around the last vestiges of self-doubt that had haunted her throughout her college career. "When Lynne had my résumé in her hand and said 'Is this all you've done?' I didn't know what she meant," winced Anderson during a 1991 conversation not long after *Absent Friends* began its run. "I thought I had done a lot. But once I was hired, a big fear of mine was letting Lynne down. She was taking a big risk by casting me, and I didn't want her to find out she had made a mistake."

But, as rehearsals progressed at an accelerated pace toward a January 1991 curtain call, Meadow, in a 1991 conversation, found her risky casting of Anderson in the pivotal role of Evelyn to be the right one. "I didn't realize we would find someone quite this green. But it is one of those great stories, where someone is cast purely on ability. Gillian's background is largely improvisational, and she worked those instincts into a highly technical style that fit in perfectly with the specific way the play was written."

The buzz on *Absent Friends* and its complete unknown in a lead role led to a packed house on opening night. And as Anderson waited backstage for her off-Broadway debut, she remembers her stomach was doing flip-flops. "I felt like somebody had shot crystal methedrine into my arm. It was physical. I was shaking and I just wanted to get off the stage. I realized I had lines, but I was just going blank. Then, all of a sudden, autopilot took over."

Absent Friends ran sixty-four performances and initially earned Anderson some good, if not spectacular, notices. *The New Yorker* noted, "Gillian Anderson is exactly right as the sullen Evelyn," while New York applauded the "respectable acting of Gillian Anderson."

Anderson's acting skills continued to progress as *Absent Friends* continued to play to packed houses, and by the time the curtain rang down for the final time on March 15, 1991, the unknown actress was on the fast track that would result in her winning the coveted Theatre World Award. Anderson took the award with grace, but in a 1991 conversation, she seemed more concerned with the realities of the acting life. "Staying employed is every actor's concern. There is a slight fear that this will be my first and last job for a while. But that's in every actor's mind as long as they live. I tend to have a great deal of faith that, wherever my life goes, it will be the best thing for me."

The actress's fears proved unfounded, for

shortly after *Absent Friends* closed, she was faced with three simultaneous offers. One was a no-budget film of questionable worth, another was an interesting turn in a small dramatic feature called *The Turning*, and the third was the offer to do the play *The Philanthropist* at the famed Long Wharf Theatre in New Haven, Connecticut. Gillian and her agent put their heads together. The no-budget film was eliminated, and because *The Philanthropist* was willing to wait, in late 1991 Anderson went to the Appalachian Mountains in Virginia to do *The Turning*.

Anderson's choices at the earliest of points in her career were indicative of her freewheeling attitude and willingness to take chances particularly because, at this point, her agents were regularly advising her to leave the highbrow East Coast and go to Los Angeles to do the TV guest shot/small-movie-part hustle. Anderson, still very much the artist in her own head, steadfastly refused and, in fact, relished the unknown quantity that *The Turning* represented.

The Turning, directed and written by Lou Puopolo and starring Karen Allen,

Tess Harper, and Michael Dolan, tells the tale of a dysfunctional family in the outback of Pocahontas, Virginia, and the return of their extreme right-wing son, who comes back from several years on an odyssey of self-discovery to try to put his family back together. Anderson, for her part, plays the wayward son's winsome former high school sweetheart, April Cavanaugh, whose actions (including some fleeting, tasteful nude scenes) prove critical to the film's dramatic conclusion.

Director Puopolo went bicoastal in casting the film but recalls being mighty impressed with Gillian's initial reading. "Gillian came to the casting call just like a lot of other actresses did," he recalls. "I was not a big theater person, so I did not have a clue as to her rising notoriety. For me, she was just another actress. But all that changed when she read that first time. She was right for the part and her attitude was absolutely right. She had the depth of talent, the right look, and the attitude was definitely there."

And that attitude was definitely there during the first hectic ten days of November 1991 when filming commenced in the snow-covered real-life town of Pocahontas, Virginia. "Gillian definitely came to work," explains Puopolo. "She understood her character, she listened, and she didn't throw a tantrum like a lot of actors would have under the conditions we started out with on that film. Things were constantly changing, and I was sometimes up until four in the morning rewriting the script and then bringing the fresh dialogue right onto the set. But she would pick up her new pages, learn them, and be ready to go. For me she was a true professional."

Rather than live and breathe *The Turning*, Anderson and her costars chose to live in a bed-and-breakfast in a nearby town where the actress spent her off-hours shopping for knickknacks, eating at the local diners, and basically, according to Puopolo, showing her true colors. "It could have been a real touchy situation," he explains, "because in those small towns people are real sensitive to outsiders coming to their town and being phony. From all reports she was quite real and honest in dealing with them."

The Turning finished principal photography in early December 1991, and Anderson immediately went north to begin preparation for *The Philanthropist.* Unfortunately, *The Turning* remains, to a large extent, yet another of Hollywood's casualties. *The Turning* did receive a theatrical release in Europe in 1992 but, to date, has not found a U.S. distributor. Consequently, laments the director, Anderson's very first film role has rarely been seen. "And it's too bad because she did a very good job in the film."

A post-Christmas cold snap is buffeting the New Haven, Connecticut, area just days before the Long Wharf Theatre production of *The Philanthropist* has its New Year's Eve debut. On stage the cast is going through one of its final run-throughs under the watchful eye of veteran director Gordon Edelstein.

The scene unfolding is a tense one as the character of sex-crazed Araminta is throwing herself at bookish Philip. In the meantime, Celia, Philip's fiancée (played by Anderson), is about to succumb to the seductive charms of arrogant writer Braham. As rehearsal for the scene comes to its conclusion, Celia turns as she is about to leave with Braham and looks in the direction of Philip. What director Edelstein saw that night, and would continue to see for the run of the play, is something that he has never forgotten. "That look in her eyes," recalls Edelstein with obvious relish. "It was so vulnerable and heartbreaking. But that was Gillian, she was always emotionally available for whatever was called for."

Like everybody else at this point, Edelstein was largely clueless about Anderson. "I had been hearing a lot of things secondhand about Gillian. I knew she had done *Absent Friends* in New York and that she was quite wonderful in it. But that was about it. But our casting director, Debra Brown, was pretty high on her and so we brought her in."

Edelstein was not sorry. "She was unbelievable. She was incredibly real and enormously convincing, and a big thing in her favor, seeing as how this was a British play, was that she could speak with an impeccable British accent." The director, who claims to normally "lose a lot of sleep and basically go bananas" during the casting process, had no such problems as Anderson finished her audition, was given the standard "we'll be in touch," and left the audition area.

"Gillian left the room and I immediately turned to Debra and said, 'Wow! This woman is unbelievable!' I said, 'She's like a force of nature. Does she want to do it?' Debra said, 'I don't know.' I said, 'Well go after her!' Debra immediately ran down the hall after her. From where I stood, I could hear Gillian walking down the stairs and about to get into the elevator and Debra yelling, 'Oh Gillian!' I didn't hear the rest of the conversation, but Debra came back, moments later, and said she would do it. I said, 'Then I think we ought to go ahead and offer it to her.'"

They did and she did. In hindsight, Anderson's decision should come as no surprise. Inclined at this point toward a theater career, Anderson felt, in her more insecure moments, that perhaps *Absent Friends* had been a fluke and that a second role in an equally ambitious production would validate her skills in her own mind as well as the mind of critics.

Ronald Guttman, one of Anderson's co-stars in *The Philanthropist*, recalls being charmed by Anderson during those first rehearsals. "My initial impressions of Gillian were that she appeared very European in the sense that she was very anchored in text and literature. She was always smoking, always reading, and always drinking coffee, which was a very European thing to do. That gave us a kind of kinship. Gillian also came across as being charming and flirtatious in a nice sort of way," the actor continues. "She had a seductress quality about her that was also quite sweet and friendly."

Tim Choate, another cast member, saw a slightly different side of her. Like Guttman, he praises Anderson's acting skills and offers that she was excellent in the role of Celia. "Gillian was very reserved," he observes. "She was very guarded and closed off."

The Philanthropist ran through February 9, 1992, and received mixed to very good reviews. Anderson, once again, proved a darling with the critics. The *Hartford Courant* proclaimed that "Gillian Anderson's Celia displays a hard baby face to the world as she brutally cuts down all the dons who have tried to have their way with her." The *Manchester Journal Inquirer* stated that "Anderson's Celia is equal parts disarming charm and selfishness."

Guttman is not surprised at the critical praise Anderson received. "When we were on stage, she would totally be there in the moment. Gillian never gave me the feeling that she was acting by rote. When I would look at her on stage, I knew I would be getting something back."

When not performing, Anderson would occasionally go into New York to see a play or hang out in New Haven with the rest of the cast. Edelstein recalls that when she was not performing, he saw glimpses of a budding maternal instinct in the actress that would blossom in later years. "Occasionally Gillian would come to my home to visit and she would immediately get down on the floor and play with my daughter. You could see that she had a special rapport with children." And those moments, he claims, indicated a more mature person than the one in those troubled teen stories he had heard over the years. "Gillian had a real centered, spiritual side to her. She could be quiet but she also had her funny and flamboyant sides as well."

It was during this period that Anderson

developed a love relationship with costar Choate. Up until that point Anderson would regularly spout the traditional theater line "I will never go to Los Angeles." She reveals, "I always felt there was a feeling of falseness in Los Angeles. It was like they really didn't care for the creative process there, just about box office, money, and power. I was somewhat pigheaded about that. Television represented a step down or a sellout to me at that point. At that time, avoiding television at all costs was something I felt very strongly about." Costar Guttman tended to take her at her word. "She seemed to love working in the theater and I believe she was planning on returning to New York after the run of *The Philanthropist* and remaining in theater."

But her professional integrity soon ran afoul of affairs of the heart, for when *The Philanthropist* ended its run and Choate left the East Coast for Los Angeles, Gillian pined away for only a short time before she bought herself a ticket for LA, too.

five

ãOH MY GOD!ä

GILLIAN ANDERSON ARRIVED IN LOS ANGELES early in 1992. Although her agent had long been suggesting that she relocate for professional reasons, Anderson recalled in a 1994 interview that the original reason for the trip was purely personal. “I came out to Los Angeles to visit a man I had met in the play I did in New Haven,” recalls Anderson, who in all interviews has kept the particulars of this liaison hush-hush. “I had only planned on staying for two weeks. But I got here and immediately sold my return ticket.”

Anderson and Tim Choate’s relationship continued in that emotional, occasionally bumpy way when creative people mix love and other passions. In the beginning it was good, so good that Anderson, early on, was in danger of both falling in love with the very Los Angeles lifestyle she detested and forgetting about her art. However, she could not keep from scratching the itch for too long. Deciding to mix business with pleasure, Gillian told her agent she was ready to work. On her terms. "I did not come to Los Angeles to do television," she once said. "I only wanted to do films."

Unfortunately, for the next year, Anderson's East Coast reputation only translated to yet another out-of-work actress on the streets of Hollywood. Although she exaggerates that she "went on three or four film auditions a day for a year," Gillian was actually going out for auditions rarely and batting zero. "I couldn't get anything," she related with obvious discomfort in 1994. "I didn't have any money and I was relying on my boyfriend to help me out financially."

Choate, who was reluctant to discuss "anything that was personal between us," did verify that Anderson was in a major-league slump. "She hustled very hard. It was tough to watch her struggle. She went out on a lot of auditions and was just not getting anything."

One near miss that remains in Anderson's memory was the role of fourteen-year-old Caril Ann Fugate in the television movie *Murder in the Heartland* about mass murderer Charles Starkweather. Anderson, in easily one of her toughest acting challenges to date, impressed the producers with her ability to play a dysfunctional teen with a homicidal bent. She ultimately lost the role but claims the experience as a moral victory. "It was neat and inspiring, at a time when I wasn't getting much work, to be considered for a role like that."

Reluctantly Anderson lowered her sights and agreed when "my picky agent and manager" began sending her on auditions for television guest shots. But Anderson continued to be bedeviled by what she considered a lack of meaningful work. One such less-than-meaningful offer came her way in 1993 when she was chosen for the female lead of Rachel in the audiobook version of *Exit to Eden* by Ann Rampling (aka Anne Rice). "I did that tape because I desperately needed the money," she related during a 1995 interview. "I auditioned for it, got the part, and then flew to New York to record it. I did a first read-through with the actor playing the male lead, and we discovered that we had to come up with all these different accents and voices. My initial thought was, 'God! What have I gotten myself into?' Eventually we just went into the studio and winged it. It was just a matter of diving in head first and hoping I would not end up doing something that would embarrass myself."

Anderson survived that trial by fire and ultimately landed her very first television role, as a troubled college student in an episode ("The Accused") of the short-lived 1993 series *Class of '96*. "I did it. It was a paycheck. But it really didn't lead to anything."

Anderson, at this point, was in a self-destructive phase, owing perhaps to the fact that her relationship with Choate was getting a bit rocky. "It was getting to the point where I began going in for some auditions that I would pray that I would not get because I didn't want to be involved in it." Until three months later when her agent rang her up with the offer to audition for something called *The X-Files*.

The X-Files was conceived sometime in the early months of 1992 by former surfing-magazine editor, screenwriter, and freelance journalist Chris Carter. "From the outset, I wanted to create a very scary show," he declares of the early goals he set for *The X-Files*. "I wanted the show to possess more broad and frightening stories than simply here's the monster of the week. And I knew the show would be a long shot because, even in the early stages, I felt our strengths would be the type of stories people had never seen before and the fact that we would be casting unknowns in the leads."

Carter, who drew much of his inspiration for this concept of FBI investigators on cases involving the likes of aliens, liver eaters, and all manner of paranormal activity from the short-lived 1970s TV series *Kolchak: The Night Stalker,* also had another classic show, *The Avengers,* in mind when he was drawing up the characters and the relationship of Special Agents Fox Mulder and Dana Scully. "I loved the relationship in that show," Carter recalls. "It was everything a man and woman could have together without being involved romantically. They worked well together, they were friendly, and it was all strictly platonic. That's what I wanted for Mulder and Scully."

Carter also wanted his characters to have legitimate, believable, very 1990s kinds of backstories. Consequently, anyone who came across the early breakdown on the character of Agent Dana Scully was surprised by how detailed it was.

Dana Katherine Scully was born on February 23, 1964, birthplace unknown, to William Scully (a career navy captain) and Margaret Scully. Scully was the third of four children (an older brother, William Scully, Jr., an older sister, Melissa Scully, and a younger brother, Charles Scully).

Scully attended the University of California at Berkeley for one year where her straightforward, logical approach to her intended forensic medicine and pathology major was tempered by a brush with political activism, her participation on the fringes of anti–nuclear war groups on campus. Scully transferred to the University of Maryland the next year and continued her education.

Scully was recruited by the FBI directly out of medical school in 1986. Scully, who earned an undergraduate degree in physics at the University of Maryland, came to the bureau's attention largely on the strength of her senior thesis, titled "Einstein's Twin Paradox: A New Interpretation." She taught for two years at Quantico Academy before being assigned to the X-Files by FBI section chief Scott Blevins. Scully's assignment, initially at least, was to shadow special agent Fox Mulder with the ultimate goal of debunking the entire project.

Special Agent Scully, ID No. 2317-616, lives in a small functional apartment at 3170 West 53rd Road #35 in Annapolis, Maryland. Her office telephone number is (202) 555-6431. Her E-mail address is D Scully@FBI.gov. Her weapon of choice is a Smith and Wesson 1056, which uses 9 mm rounds.

Knowing that the success of *The X-Files* would ultimately hinge on the relationship between Mulder and Scully, Carter was prepared to "go through a long and tedious casting process. I knew finding the right people was going to be tough."

The Fox network turned thumbs up on Carter's *X-Files* in August 1992. The final draft of the pilot script was turned in on December 12, 1992. During the writing process, the name *Mulder* was borrowed from Carter's mother's maiden name and *Scully* came courtesy of baseball announcer Vin Scully. An important decision made during the writing of the script, and one that would have a strong impact on Anderson's interpretation of the character, was to eliminate from the script Scully's apparent, active romantic life with lobbyist Ethan Minette (and a scene where Scully and Minette are in bed together) in favor of a more story-driven and from Anderson's point of view a "noninvolved" premise for the show.

Of course Anderson did not have an inkling that any of this was going on. "It had been about a year since I had worked in anything, so that would have definitely influenced my decision at that point. At that point I was willing to go along for the ride if there was a paycheck involved. . . . I was going out on a lot of auditions and

X-Files came up, and it seemed, at first, just like any other television stuff. But, when I read the pilot script, I saw that it was an intriguing and pretty intense story line. I also tend to lean toward this kind of subject matter. I've always been a full-fledged believer in psychics, UFOs, and ghosts and things. But what really sold me was the fact that for the first time in a long time I was reading something that involved a strong, independent, intelligent woman as a lead character. I also saw something in the relationship between Mulder and Scully that was compelling and interesting. I felt that the dynamics and tension between the two characters was wonderful."

The irony of the Dana Scully character was also not lost on Anderson. For, although Scully is a nonbeliever to the *n*th degree, Anderson has always had an affinity and belief in all things paranormal. Books on spiritual topics have long been a large part of her library. She has admitted, on more than one occasion, to consulting psychics and has been known to turn to tarot cards for guidance. "I've been fascinated by the supernatural since I was a child," she confesses. "And as far as UFOs go, well, I know we are not alone. I'd like to see an alien very much. It seems so likely that there is something other than us in this universe."

Anderson went in for her first audition for *The X-Files* and, perhaps in a nod to her now distant punk days, was hardly dressed for success. "It didn't help matters when I went in for that first audition wearing a borrowed suit that was very baggy on me. The casting director took one look at me and said I was frumpy." Anderson remembered that situation in 1996 not as an attempt to shoot herself in the foot but instead as part and parcel of her lackadaisical attitude toward personal grooming. "I honestly don't look in the mirror much," she admits. "I get up in the morning and, most of the time, I get to work and have my hair and makeup done before I realize I should have checked to see if I had sleep in my eyes."

Still, Anderson made enough of an impression to be called back a few days later to meet with Carter and the other *X-Files* producers. This time the actress walked in wearing a borrowed suit that was a better fit and some moderately high heels. It was a definite improvement but Carter was not amused. "She came in looking a little disheveled, a little grungier than I imagined Scully being," Carter remembers. "But you could not miss those classic features. And she had a seriousness about her and real believability about her. I believed her when she spoke scientific terms. I believed her as a doctor. I think she looked the part and she did not look like your typical TV bombshell."

Anderson, for her part, recalls that audition as being very intense. "When I went in for the pilot audition, it was very obvious that Chris Carter had a real strong, concrete idea of who Scully was, and he guided me through whenever he felt I was getting off track. It was very clear to him who she was, and, I guess, Chris saw some of those elements in me when I auditioned. But what Chris ultimately saw in me, well, I'm not really sure. I tend to have a seriousness about me and Scully is written very seriously. Scully rarely cracks a smile, and maybe that came across in the audition."

It was a very shaky Gillian Anderson

who, days later, reported to the Fox corporate towers for the latest in a series of many auditions for the network brass and the first with her soon-to-be costar David Duchovny. Carter had already made his feelings known that he was very high on Anderson for the part of Dana Scully. But the network executives, despite having no problems with her acting talents, seemed to have a big problem with her looks, as Anderson laughingly remembers now with no small sense of irony. "When the network auditions started, I wasn't sure what they wanted. But maybe I should have had a clue when they kept telling me to wear something more formfitting and smaller with higher heels. It became obvious after a time that they wanted a typical television bimbo, someone taller, leggier, and bustier. I guess they had it in their mind to make this 'The XXX-Files.'"

Duchovny, who at that point in the audition process didn't know Gillian at all and was unfamiliar with her previous work, was a quick convert to her side. "That whole thing was so overblown on the part of the network," recalled Duchovny of Anderson's audition in a 1996 interview.

"You look at Gillian and she's a beautiful woman. And besides, how often do you see Scully in a bathing suit? She not six feet tall and she doesn't have what's-her-face tits. But she's got as nice a face as any of them. I think the network's big thing was that they thought she was not tall enough or not Pamela Anderson enough."

But while the jury was definitely out on Anderson, the Fox network people were literally wetting themselves at the prospect of David Duchovny as true believer Fox Mulder. Duchovny, like Anderson, is a well-read, literate, and somewhat brooding and vulnerable-appearing actor, and had already made a name for himself in a series of quirky movie and television roles which included host of the erotic cable series *The Red Shoe Diaries,* the cross-dressing private eye in *Twin Peaks,* and the innocent caught up in the cross-country serial-killer odyssey *Kalifornia*. The at-large impression was that Duchovny was quite good though prone to being aloof. "David, in a lot of people's eyes, was considered a star and had already done a considerable amount of work, so it was easy to see his quality," reflects Carter.

"Gillian had done very little work and it was harder to convince the people whose money I was spending that she was Dana Scully."

Anderson, standing in the hallway going over her script again for yet another audition for the network, was excited that she had gotten this far and more than a little frustrated that she was fighting the network's misplaced notion of Scully as sex bomb. "I was still convinced they were looking for somebody leggier and chestier, and I obviously was not that bimbo. But it had gotten to the point where they were either going to cast me or cast somebody else."

Her old college professor, Ric Murphy, had remained close friends with Anderson after her college days. He had been in the audience when Anderson tasted her first bit of success with *Absent Friends*. And so he was not too surprised when one day he received a telephone call from his former pupil with some exciting news. "She called and warned me that things were really starting to happen for her after a very foul period in Los Angeles. I had my fingers crossed for her. She had this strong thing going for her in New York and then she had gone to LA and her career appeared to have stopped dead. So when she told me she had gone through several auditions for this thing called *The X-Files*, and that she was right on the verge, I was overjoyed."

"Hi. I'm David Duchovny."

Anderson looked up into the actor's smiling face. She smiled back and shook his outstretched hand.

"I was thinking," continues Duchovny, "it might help if we run through this scene a few times before we go in."

The pair began trading dialogue in that cold, corporate hallway, and after a few readings, the first sparks of the chemistry that would bind them together on the show began to flicker.

"It was amazing," recalls Anderson of those first exchanges. "I truly believe those moments were better than anything we've done since."

Duchovny recalls that on the day of Anderson's audition he already knew that he had the part, and so as he and Anderson stepped into the audition room, he was relaxed and even a little cocky. "This was my room, this was my part," he relates, "and so I played the scene in a kind of sarcastic way, and Gillian was completely thrown by it. She was shocked that anyone would talk to her that way. And that's exactly how she should have reacted. It was perfect."

But there were still the network executives to convince, and despite a solid reading that day, the suits at the top were still not quite willing to commit to Anderson. It remained for Chris Carter to call their bluff shortly after Anderson and Duchovny left the room. "I stood up," recalls Carter, "and said quite loudly that I did not want another actress in the part. I wanted Gillian."

Carter knew he was putting his butt on the line. He did not have anything approaching a track record that would allow him to make this kind of ultimatum, and he knew that shows and, in his case, a budding career had been derailed for a lot less bravado than he was showing. There were tense moments of silence. Then smiles slowly began to crack on the executives' faces.

"They picked me," recalls Anderson, "and, to be perfectly honest, I was surprised. No, let me rephrase that. I was shockingly surprised."

No more surprised than when she went home that day and discovered, among the assorted junk mail and bills, her very last unemployment check. Gillian Anderson was officially off the dole. And *The X-Files* was her ticket to ride.

Anderson's relationship with Choate had long since peaked and was heading steadily toward crash and burn. But she looked back, philosophically, on the events surrounding the relationship. "I could have ended the relationship, stayed in New York, and never gone to Los Angeles. But, if I had not made the choices I made to be with that person, I never would have given myself the choices and opportunities that led to my getting *The X-Files*."

Consequently, there was nothing and no one to tie her to Los Angeles when she discovered that *The X-Files* would be filming in Vancouver, Canada, in a series of block house–looking sound stages that went under the name North Shores Studios. Her next ten months would consist of fifteen-hour shooting days and nights in weather that would rarely be accommodating.

Throw in the fact that shooting the pilot, midway through 1993, represented only the fourth time Anderson had ever acted in front of a camera, and it was a safe bet that the visible shakes she was exhibiting that first day on the set had very little to do with the cold weather. "Let me tell you about tension and stress," she recalls with more than a hint of disdain. "I got the job on *X-Files* when I was twenty-four and so I was still in a period where I was desperately trying to figure out who I was. I was a mess. I was terrified. I didn't know what I was doing. I didn't know what hitting the mark was, and I didn't know anything about making a television program. I didn't know much about what a pilot was, and I just automatically assumed that after we made the pilot, we would be picked up as a series. I was so naive and in the dark about so much of what we were doing. Fortunately, David was there to take me under his wing. His reassurance meant a lot to me because it was a very scary time."

Indeed, Anderson was having her problems as the first days of filming rolled out in Vancouver. It was not uncommon in those early days to have numerous takes on a relatively simple scene because she had not hit her mark or had mishandled a prop. "I was still trying to formulate who Scully was in my own mind. I was also very paranoid. Every time the producers and director would huddle for a meeting, I was convinced they were getting ready to fire me."

Anderson, the rawest of raw rookies whose training had been in theater, was, inexplicably, also having a hard time remembering her lines. Malcolm Marsden, a hairdresser on the show, recalls, "[that] upset David because he was so accomplished, had worked in feature films, and could remember his lines. But I knew he appreciated how hard she was working."

It soon became evident to crew and cast members that the stars of *The X-Files* were coming from two different points of view. Both Anderson and Duchovny, according to those who deal with them on a daily basis, were immediately earmarked as two bright individuals whose personalities made them a joy to be around. It also did not hurt that when a director yelled "Action!" they were both quite professional as well.

Director Jerrold Freedman, who put the

actors through their paces during the first season episodes "Ghost in the Machine" and "Born Again," saw Duchovny as somebody you talk to about a million things. "Gillian, on the other hand, was always very focused on her character and what she was doing. She's constantly pushing herself to work harder and harder as an actress. She took direction very well and she asked all the right questions."

Carter's confidence in Anderson's abilities never wavered, but just before filming began, he did make one cosmetic decision that to this day has the actress busting up with laughter. "He said my birthmark had to go," Anderson chuckles of the daily makeup job that renders the spot on her lip invisible. "Chris felt there was not enough room for it on my face."

The pilot episode, titled simply "The X-Files," used the premise of mysterious teen deaths and their possible link to alien experimentation to introduce lone wolf Mulder and his newly assigned partner, the cool, calm, and very logical Dana Scully. Fairly early in the pilot, Anderson quickly adjusted to the rigors of what Duchovny early on described as "lots of motels, too many dark woods, and it always seems to be in the middle of the night."

It was at the end of a long day and night of shooting in the middle of nowhere for a sequence in which Mulder and Scully are dealing with the unknown in the middle of a driving rainstorm. The rain, courtesy of a nearby water cannon, had been playing on the actors for hours, and Duchovny, soaked to the skin, visibly shivering, and very tired, had a look in his eyes that said "Take me home" in capital letters. But not everyone was ready to pack it in.

"It was a little unreal," recalls Duchovny in his patented understated tones. "She was standing in the middle of all this, wanting to be colder and wetter. At one point, she actually turned her face right into the rain machine, saying, 'Hit me with more water!'"

The actress, who prided herself on being in good shape physically, didn't blink twice when the pilot called for action. "From the beginning I was really up to do my own tumbles." One thing she had to learn on the job was the handling of firearms, which was completely foreign to her. "It felt very awkward in the beginning," Anderson reflects. "I didn't even know how to hold a gun, and so initially my hand would practically cover the whole thing. I had to be reminded not to do that."

Anderson's quick study of the Dana Scully character was so complete that when a scene in the pilot episode called for her to enter Mulder's motel room dressed in somewhat revealing night clothes so that he could examine strange marks on her back, which turned out to be mosquito bites, she complied, all the while knowing that the parameters of *The X-Files* and her character would never allow such a scene to exist. "At that point it was the pilot, it was my first job, and that's how the scene was written," recalls Anderson with a nervous laugh. "There really wasn't a reason for the scene to be played that way and for me to have to appear in my underwear. The bites could have just as easily been on my shoulder. But that was a one-time situation. I don't see that kind of thing happening again."

Carter, immediately aware of people reading more into that scene than was actually there, explains that "the scene in the motel room was deliberate. It was my way of letting people know that the relationship between Mulder and Scully was going to be platonic." Anderson's nagging fear that, when all was said and done, she would still end up being a tart disappeared almost immediately when in "Deep Throat," the second episode, Scully pulls a gun on a security agent and hollers, "Hands on the car! Do it! Do it! Do it!" "I wanted Scully to be Mulder's equal in every way," explains Carter of his reason for letting Scully get tough so early in the show's life. "It was important to me that the audience get the point that she would never need his help."

Anderson and Duchovny, in the "Deep Throat" episode, also got on-the-spot training on just how rigorous doing *The X-Files* was going to be. "We were supposed to be standing out in the middle of nowhere, watching as these UFOs rise up on the horizon and separate," she recalls. "It was two o'clock on this really drizzly morning and the director was running up and down saying things like 'Okay, they're moving up! They're coming toward you! You're amazed!' And we were going crazy, going cross-eyed trying to adjust our sight lines to what was going on." In fact, "Deep

Throat," for Anderson, epitomized the technical difficulties in TV making that the novice actress admits to having a tough time learning. "There was much to learn on the technical side, especially when it came to things like reaction shots. Also, ninety-nine point nine percent of each episode is shot out of sequence. So, when we received each script, we had to understand the various psychological, intellectual, and emotional states of our characters."

All through preproduction, Carter and company continued to struggle with how much of a social/romantic life Agent Scully should have. What they decided was that she should have none, and they did away with it in the episode "The Jersey Devil." In hindsight a rather tepid take on the whole Bigfoot legend, "The Jersey Devil" did allow Scully one last date before she decided that dealing with the wacky world of Fox Mulder was going to be a full-time job. Anderson, who gave that element of the show high marks, did concede that "it would be interesting to see Scully play to that side and to see her date and to explore her private life. But I do think it's appropriate for this particular show not to delve

Photo credit: T. Charles Erickson

Gillian as Celia in a scene from Long Wharf Theatre's production of *The Philanthropist* by Christopher Hampton.

Photo credit: John Paschal—Celebrity Photo

Gillian and her (now estranged) husband Errol Clyde Klotz holding hands at the 1995 Golden Globes awards show.

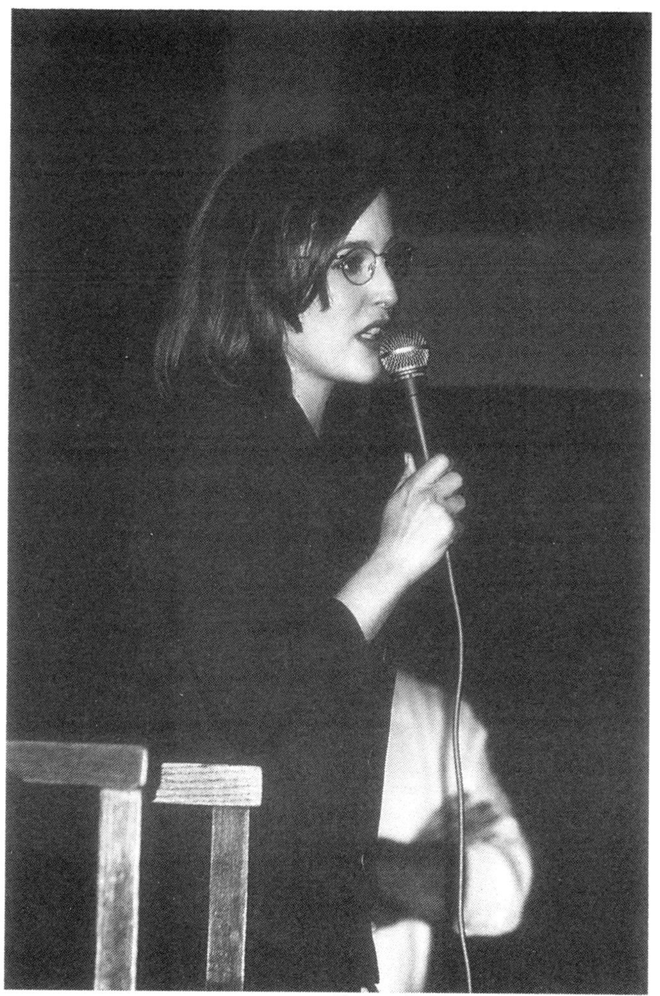

Photo credit: Albert Ortega—Celebrity Photo

Gillian is holding court during her one and only *X-Files* convention appearance in 1996.

Photo credit: Scott Downie—Celebrity Photo

Gillian and her *X-Files* co-star David Duchovny are out of their paranormal element during a 1996 party in Los Angeles.

Photo credit: Scott Downie—Celebrity Photo

It's a meeting of the metal minds as Anderson, Duchovny and *X-Files* creator Chris Carter mingle with alternative heavy metal rockers Glenn Danzig and Rob Zombie.

Gillian races through LAX and back home following her appearance at the 1996 Emmy Awards.

Photo credit: John Paschal—Celebrity Photo

Gillian and David at the Emmy Awards, where Anderson accepted the adoration of fans for her Best Actress nomination.

Photo credit: Scott Downie—Celebrity Photo

Gillian with the true love of her life, the Flukeman monster from the episode “The Host,” at a 1996 party honoring *The X-Files*.

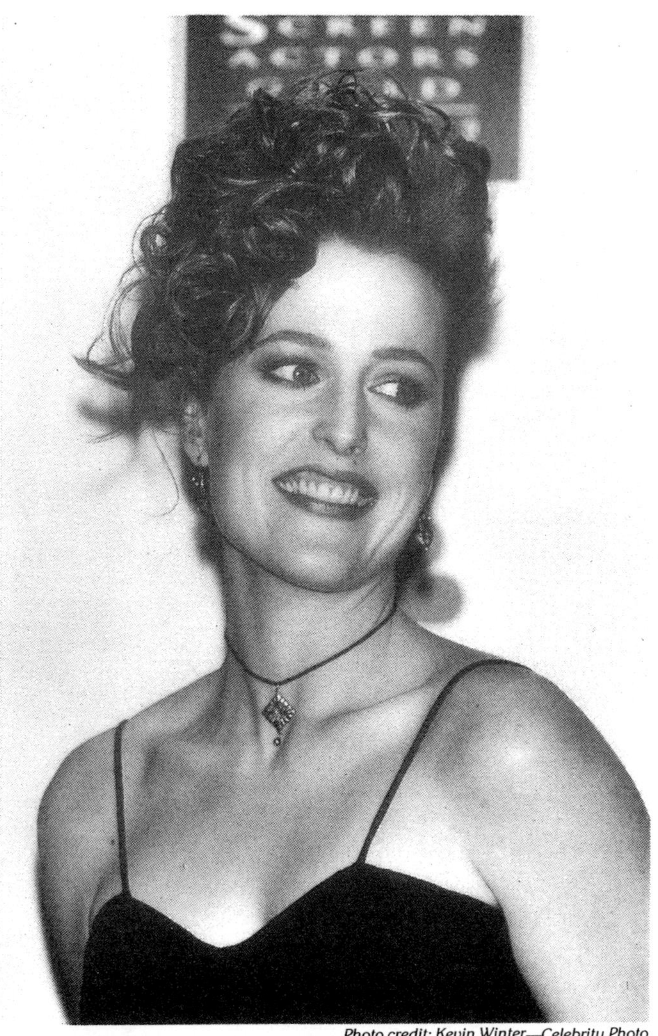

Photo credit: Kevin Winter—Celebrity Photo

Gillian Anderson, looking radiant and very unlike Scully, at the 1996 Screen Actors' Guild awards show.

into their personal lives. There isn't room with everything that happens in each episode every week for the writers to enter into our private lives. That would mean a whole twenty minutes that would need to be devoted to it in one way or another. And there just isn't the time to do that."

The X-Files premiered on September 10, 1993. Although the show, despite the expected low ratings associated with a network that had far fewer stations than other networks, took up residence near the bottom of the TV ratings, *The X-Files* settled almost immediately into a comfortable Friday night habit for the science-fiction crowd. For those involved in its creation, and particularly for Anderson, *The X-Files* was still in the growth stage. And one of the things Anderson, always an expressive actress even when the story required otherwise, had to learn was an extremely low-key style of acting that seemed to go hand in hand with the series' bleak storytelling landscape. "Admittedly playing things this low key is not my style," recalls Anderson, looking back on the voyage of discovery that was *The X-Files'* first season. "It was always hinted at in the scripts. The lines were written very deadpan. I think David and I both kind of settled into underplaying things as we worked together, and by doing it so often, it has become a recognizable part of the show."

"Ice," the episode in which Mulder and Scully find themselves trapped in an Arctic research station with a parasite that may or may not be affecting them, was the first truly terrifying moment in the series and contains a real shock to the system—the first time Mulder and Scully point a gun at each other. "I think that show was one of the first turning points for us," remembers the actress. "There was a feeling of panic that swept through the episode, and as actors, that was an interesting emotion to play. There was also a bitter conflict between Mulder and Scully. He wants to preserve the creature and study it, and I want to kill it straightaway. I felt the scene where Mulder and Scully confront each other was a real jolt to their relationship."

A jolt to Gillian Anderson's acting world-view was the amount of physical work *The X-Files* required. It was not uncommon for Anderson to spend a good chunk of each episode running, drawing weapons, or being roughed up. After a particularly rough-and-tumble day on the set, Anderson recalls that she discovered "all kinds of black and blue marks."

It was becoming apparent midway through the first season that the show's writers had become real Gillian Anderson fans and, consequently, were working juicy bits of Scully business into just about every episode. In "Fire," Scully got to dance on the fringes of jealousy when an old flame of Mulder's turns up. "Beyond the Sea" allowed Scully the anguish of dealing with the loss of her father while locking horns with a death-row inmate in a very *Silence of the Lambs* à la Jodie Foster way. In the creepy shape-shifting saga "Genderbender," Scully is nearly sexually assaulted by an Amish alien.

Anderson, reflecting on the series shortly after the completion of the episode "Lazarus," in which a former lover of Scully's is killed and comes back from the dead, and Scully is abducted for the first of what will be many times during the run of the series, allowed, "At first I was just kind of thrown into this. As I've gotten used to the way television works, I've certainly changed Scully a bit."

Working in relative isolation, it was inevitable that the cast and crew would quickly become like a family. It was also inevitable that Anderson would mix socially with them. But even Anderson could not have envisioned what happened the day she met the show's production designer, Errol Clyde Klotz.

Their relationship started with the expected small talk, but Klotz remembers that things moved beyond the friendship stage very quickly. "Gillian was a very spiritual person. I could tell that right away. There was also a kind of immediate, unspoken connection between us. We felt like we had known each other a long time and we had just finally met in person."

Anderson and Klotz immediately became an item, spending all their free time together—which, admittedly, was not much as *The X-Files* became a treadmill with Anderson and Duchovny wrapping up one episode on a Friday and literally being handed a brand-new script that they would have to memorize by the following Monday.

As Gillian Anderson's real-life romance

heated up, so too did the first sparks of controversy over when Mulder and Scully would hit the sheets. As evidenced by the episode “The Jersey Devil,” Scully decides to forgo a personal life in favor of a professional and never boring life with Mulder. Carter, looking back on that episode, waxes philosophical on what Scully’s last date meant to the evolving nature of the show. “It was a moment that showed how time passes, decisions are made, and people move on with their lives.” But, with Scully symbolically free at the conclusion of “The Jersey Devil,” all concerned immediately defused any possibility of the two agents suddenly getting physical. “The show’s not about that,” recalled Anderson, who was already tired of addressing that issue, in a 1994 interview. “It’s about our cases and our professional relationship. If we establish a romantic relationship, it would distract from the main theme of the show and everything would just kind of go downhill. There’s a big concern about keeping us platonic.”

Duchovny, during a first-season conversation, agrees with the notion that the show was taking the creative high road by not immediately linking Mulder and Scully romantically. "Having a friendship and a professional working relationship with a woman is much more interesting, and I'm sure Gillian would tell you the same thing. It's very easy to just jump into bed. That doesn't take much imagination." This lack of imagination was apparently demonstrated by Fox network executives because, according to writer James Wong, "The first question Fox studio executives wanted answered about the two leads was 'When are they going to go to bed?' And the answer, states show producer Howard Gordon, is when pigs fly. "The show established early on that these are two people who care about each other but also respect each other. A Scully and Mulder romance? Not in this plane. I think everybody knows that as soon as they share a bed it's all over for them, and most likely, it would be all over for the show."

In lieu of overt sexual tension, *The X-Files* continued to put Scully through a myriad of other emotional hoops. One of the most stirring of these manifested itself in the episode "Miracle Man," a tale of a young faith healer suspected of not doing good works, which had as a subtle subtext the normally cold and scientifically calculating Agent Scully confronting her own sense of spirituality. "They've definitely begun to explore more of Scully's spirituality over the past year," reflects Anderson, who admits that playing Scully's science side has always been difficult given her own tendency to believe in the unbelievable. "It's interesting to play somebody so totally committed to her own beliefs who has them suddenly altered by what she has seen and experienced."

But the actress's assessment of her first season's portrayal of Agent Scully indicates that she's still facing some ongoing challenges. "A lot of what I'm doing on this show is just so totally pretending. When Scully is angry or afraid, I can draw on experience. But when I'm dealing with things like alien encounters and shape-shifting serial killers, then it's up to my imagination. Dialogue on this show is also very tough. Because it's so technical, it's often hard to memorize and even more difficult to verbalize in an interesting way."

Anderson's opinion that her alter ego was changing on an almost weekly basis seemed to be confirmed when the episodes "Darkness Falls," "Tooms," "Born Again," and "Roland" whizzed by in a blur of added dimensions and deeper character emotions. For a lead role in a weekly television series, Anderson felt she had captured the gold ring. "The relationship between Mulder and Scully is getting stronger and stronger all the time," she assesses. "It's been a natural progression. It's not something I've worked on. It's just been this path I've been on."

Anderson put a thoughtful spin on the inevitable and, by this time, already annoying question of when Mulder and Scully would hit the sheets. "There's a tension between the two characters that is right out of a 1940s movie," she explains. "If you look closely at what we've done to this point, you can see that we've done some incredibly intimate things that have nothing to do with sex. So Mulder and Scully's first touch in an episode becomes that much more exciting. If we got in the sack together, the holding of hands and the intimate touches would mean nothing." Her serious tone lightens, and she has a good laugh at the notion that Scully has thought about Mulder in "that way." "I think there have been times when she has been completely charmed and touched by him. But I don't know if she's ever really imagined him naked."

At their most optimistic, the show's producers could not have imagined a more balanced off-screen chemistry developing between Anderson and Duchovny. Duchovny's dry wit and often-perceived sullen, quiet nature would seem forever on a collision course with Anderson's more emotional and almost childlike naivete and enthusiasm. Duchovny was a polished professional. Anderson was largely inexperienced and still prone to rookie mistakes. In fact, people were so on the lookout for the inevitable blowup that the very sturdy bond that was developing between the two actors was not something that was immediately evident during the show's inaugural season. But, as observant crew people will tell, a sort of shorthand had, by the second season, become a very real element of their professional relationship. Few words seem to pass between them. But they are the right words because the pair always appears in a state of professional grace—

very focused, very relaxed, and according to comments offered by wardrobe supervisor Gillian Kieft in 1995, very aware of each other's moods and needs. "The way Mulder and Scully are on screen is the way David and Gillian are in person," she says. "They help each other and they respect each other." And it is a relationship based largely on the fact that when the workday is over, they go their separate ways. "No, we don't hang out," Duchovny offered in a 1995 interview. "We are very wary of the fact that, at any moment, the other person can turn into a psychotic human being because of the demands that are put on us. I know when she is very tired and irritable, and she knows the same about me. We have a great respect for the fine line the other is walking all the time."

Despite the very together nature of the Klotz-Anderson relationship, the rumors inevitably hit the tabloids that Anderson and Duchovny were romantically involved. The actors were quick to deny it, the collective consensus being that they would both be fired from the show if the rumors were true and that Carter would not think twice about ending the show rather than letting off-screen passion screw up his carefully conceived on-screen relationship between Agents Mulder and Scully.

Anderson's rapid maturity as an actress in general and in the role of Scully in particular continued to be a pleasant surprise to even the most skeptical cast and crew members. For director David Nutter, who was there from the beginning and has directed in excess of fourteen episodes, the actress's progress has been unbelievable. "I've been very moved and, in some cases, touched by her ability to be very honest and to be able to tell the truth in emotional scenes," he says.

Anderson's relationship with Klotz continued to move at high speed. But not even she was prepared for the bit of *X-Files* strangeness that entered her personal life late in 1993 when, at a Southern California party thrown by Fox to help celebrate the success of the show, Anderson sat down with a professional psychic named Debi Becker. Becker looked at Gillian, asked a few perfunctory questions and announced, "You're going to have a little girl."

Anderson was not thrilled. "No I'm not," she said, recalling the incident in a 1995 interview. "That can't happen. I just got this show!"

Weeks later, however, after an engagement period that Anderson describes in hindsight as "lasting shorter than a month and longer than a week," Klotz and Anderson winged off to Hawaii where, on New Year's Day 1994, they married in a rather unorthodox ceremony. "I had gotten engaged once before with a ring over a fancy dinner, and it was a very uncomfortable thing," says Anderson, perhaps making a veiled reference to her relationship with Choate. "This time it was so fabulously simple. It was just one of those channel-changing moments interrupted by wedding vows. It was so spur of the moment that we had difficulty finding a minister. There was this Buddhist temple down the street from where we were staying and so we talked to this nice priest. He drove us to this golf course and showed us this spot down by the ocean. We kept the ceremony very, very small. In fact it was just the two of us and a Buddhist priest on the seventeenth hole of a golf course."

And, the newly married couple possibly conceived a child on their wedding night.

Anderson recalls not realizing she was pregnant until two months later. But she sensed something was going on. "It was weird," she relayed in a 1995 conversation. "I found myself subconsciously doodling figures. At first I didn't know what they were or what they meant. Later I realized I had been drawing embryos." She also found herself getting nauseated and fatigued, a condition she attributed to exhaustion and a bout of the flu, a malady that swept through the show's company on a fairly regular basis.

And, because Anderson did not know she was with child, she continued to unknowingly put her pregnancy at risk by participating in the everyday *X-Files* schedule. The long hours did not help, and the physical activity proved a constant, ongoing danger. Anderson shudders at the memory of what went on during the filming of the episode "Young at Heart." "I was shooting a sequence where I was being shot at by a serial killer," she remembers. "I was shooting scene after scene where I fall backwards onto my back. At one point I fell back and just missed the edge of a marble column. I didn't realize until later that I was pregnant at the time."

Although not certain she was pregnant at the time the season-ending cliff-hanger, "The Erlenmeyer Flask," was being filmed, she looks back at how the fact she was with child may have affected her performance. "At the time I was pregnant and that influenced a lot of how I played some of those scenes. I felt it was a struggle to stay in contact with who the character is. Something happens to a woman when she gets pregnant; she loses a sense of who she is. I felt like I was a different person than the one they had originally cast as Scully."

"It was a shocker," remembers Anderson of the moment she discovered she was with child. "I was worried that it would be the end of my role. Scully was supposed to be chasing bad guys, and I was going to be big and bloated and barely able to stand on my feet."

While contemplating her next move, she reflected on the accelerated pace of her life in the past year, a year she began as an unemployed actress and ended as a star of a series, married, and expecting a baby. "I didn't plan for everything to happen in one year. In the moment, these things didn't seem like they were too much. Eventually it hit me that it was too much. It was not that I shouldn't have made those decisions. It's just that now I knew I was going to have to pay for it."

The actress moped around for several days in a quiet and withdrawn state. Few people noticed the change; the rigors of *The X-Files* often produced that reaction in people. But the wheels inside Gillian Anderson's head were turning at a frantic pace as she struggled with all her conflicting emotions. She was terrified by the prospect of breaking the news to Carter. He had stuck his neck way out for her. She could only envision the worst when she dropped this little bombshell on him. But she felt she had to tell somebody.

Anderson approached David Duchovny's trailer during a break in what was turning into a particularly grueling day of filming. Duchovny had appeared tired on the set, and they were going through a rather high number of takes. This was probably not the best day to reveal her news, but Anderson was determined that it was now or never. Gillian knocked on the trailer. The door opened. Duchovny smiled and opened the door for her to come in. He assumed Anderson had come around to go over a script change. It had been a common practice. But, this day, he could see in Anderson's eyes that she had much more than the script on her mind.

"David," she stammered. "I'm pregnant."

"Oh my god!"

"He got a little pale," recalls Anderson of that moment, "and he looked like his knees were about to buckle."

There was what seemed like an eternity of silence. David, in tones not too far removed from those employed in his role as Mulder, asked Gillian, "Is it a good thing?" Anderson thought about it for a second, her eyes growing wide in a sad but determined look.

"Yes. It's a good thing."

six

A PREGNANT PAUSE

ANDERSON LEFT DUCHOVNY'S TRAILER AND WANdered slowly back toward the set. She looked at the cast and crew, smiling at some, saying hello to others. Going through her mind was concern as to how they would react. While Duchovny, as expected, was immediately supportive and comforting, he was also quietly insistent that Anderson break the news to Carter right away.

But right away quickly turned into a few weeks. Duchovny would regularly inquire about Anderson's health and, apart from Klotz, was the only one privy to the secret. He would also question her about whether she had informed Carter and, if not, when. Anderson did not have a ready answer, because as the early signs of life began growing in her belly, the actress was scared to death. But she was equally determined to do what she felt was the right thing. "When I found out I was pregnant, I was adamant that I was not going to terminate the pregnancy," reflected Anderson during an interview shortly after the birth of her child. "I knew the decision and the risk I had to make toward having the child and I knew that I could also end up losing my job over it. The way I was feeling, I knew that, even if I didn't end up losing my job over the pregnancy, I'd probably end up wishing that I had because of all the people I was going to have to confront about it."

Though these were the thoughts that Anderson kept to herself, even her husband, whose shock at his unexpected but impending fatherhood was immediately replaced by an equally strong desire for Gillian to have the child, was aware that his wife was wrestling with these issues. "We would sit around in silence and wonder 'Oh my god! What would the repercussions be," recalls Klotz of those confusing first days after the discovery that Gillian was pregnant. "I can only imagine that all the worst-case scenarios were flashing through her head. But Gillian was not the type to verbalize those kinds of things. She would not want to tempt the fates in that way."

Anderson, ever the trooper, was inclined to continue on into what would be a pivotal second season for the show, which while establishing a solid core following in the science-fiction universe was only doing passable in the bottom-line ratings department. The actress also realized that given the time line from conception to birth she would begin visibly showing early in the second season episodes and would be a very pregnant FBI agent by the eighth episode.

But first things first. Anderson had to tell Chris Carter. Then the decision would be up to him.

Reports vary wildly on what Carter's reaction was when Anderson dropped her bombshell. More than one publication reported that Carter was hopping mad. "Well, he was shocked," the actress remembers. "I don't think Chris was too happy about it."

Several sources close to the show offered, anonymously, that "Carter went ballistic. He wanted to get rid of her." But the producer-creator was quick to respond to those stories with, "I never, ever considered replacing her. It's a lie."

Still, Carter for his part was "shocked, surprised, and just a bit disappointed." However, ultimately he sided with Anderson to somehow carry on filming through the pregnancy and make it all work in a believable, *X-Files* manner. "We still hadn't written the scripts that she was going to be in once we learned of her pregnancy," he recalled in 1995. "It was a larger problem than we anticipated having to solve at that point, but that's what producers and writers do, solve problems."

Producer Howard Gordon was not unfamiliar with this sort of thing. As one of the guiding lights on the television series *Beauty and the Beast*, Gordon was faced with writing Linda Hamilton's pregnancy into the series. "And, in hindsight, I think we made a mistake in doing that. One thing was certain, Gillian really gave us a challenge when she told us she was pregnant."

While Carter, Gordon, and the rest of the show's brain trust wracked their brains trying to figure out how to logically factor Anderson's pregnancy into the show, the news media eventually got wind of it. Just as inevitably, the Hollywood trade papers and wire services were soon burning with reports that the network was upset and concerned and putting pressure on Carter to drop Anderson from the show and to recast. Carter, normally a laid-back soul, bristled at those rumors. "Part of the show's success has rested with the audience's involvement with the characters. To recast at that point, no matter what the reason, would have been a major blow to the show. I can say emphatically that recasting Scully was never something that the people at Fox tried to make me do."

But while Carter continued to deny any and all rumors, a final decision on just what to do was not forthcoming, which gave Anderson, who was already beginning to experience the wonders of morning sickness, yet another reason to lose sleep. Still feeling positive at the prospect of motherhood, Anderson, in a post-pregnancy conversation, remembers feeling frightened by what might be in store for her professional future. "The pregnancy scared a lot of people, and it certainly scared me. The show might have survived and gone on without me. Or it could have crashed and I would have been somewhat in the middle of that. It was a rough time for myself and everyone who had to deal with the issue of whether to recast or not. . . . I was ready for anything at that point. I was making a huge life decision, and it was more about the decision I was making for myself than the decision I was making for the show. I was ready to roll with whatever punches they had given me."

The pressure was definitely on. Time was fast approaching when the first batch of scripts for the second season would have to at least be in the pipeline. At one point, the idea was floated to incorporate Anderson's pregnancy into the show. It was an idea that was quickly dismissed on the grounds that a pregnant FBI agent, and consequently an FBI agent with a baby, would slow down the proceedings and was not in keeping with the overall tone of the show. An even wackier notion had everybody in stitches. "There was a rumor in the papers that Scully would somehow give birth to an alien-human baby," chuckled producer Howard Gordon in a 1995 conversation. "Of course we dismissed that idea rather quickly."

Adding pressure as to how or if to keep Anderson was the early 1995 announcement that the show's star had captured the prestigious Golden Globe Award for best actress in a television series. It was a surprise to everyone, especially Anderson, who, when her name was announced, was in an absolute daze. "I had no clue about it," she states. "I just don't get it. And ultimately I think that's good because it keeps my head small."

The issue of Gillian Anderson's pregnancy was finally resolved by ignoring it completely. Anderson would appear in the first five episodes of the new season, although on a steadily declining basis as her pregnancy progressed. Beginning with the fifth episode, "Duane Barry," Scully would be abducted by a former FBI agent whose mental derangement is hinted at as the result of having been abducted by aliens. Thus, Scully's absence could be effectively explained through the final days of Anderson's pregnancy and would, through the use of previously shot dream sequences and the like, allow her to be completely missing from only one episode before returning in "One Breath," the eighth episode.

Almost as ingenious as the story line that would keep Anderson on the show were the extraordinary lengths the writers and cameramen went to keep Scully at least somewhat active as she gained fifty-two pounds and slowed down considerably through the early part of the second season. Additionally, scenes were fitted into already completed scripts in which Scully's contributions consisted of her talking on the telephone or sitting at a computer. The actress began wearing oversized coats and jackets. At one point, on those occasions when it was absolutely vital that a non-pregnant-appearing Scully walk through camera, a stand-in was used. "There was a lot of shooting from the neck up," recalled Anderson with a laugh during a 1995 interview. "There were a lot of high angles, and I wore a lot of trenchcoats. And there was always the joke about the cameraman putting on a wide-angle lens. But, as I began to show, it became obvious that the camera was not being kind to me. When you're pregnant, your body goes through so many changes. I would look at myself on some of those early episodes and have to turn away because my face looked so round! But, given the circumstances, I had no choice but to let go of my vanity."

Though her early-season episode time was beginning to decrease dramatically, Anderson's physical presence was still required at times, so beginning with the season opener "Little Green Men," the crew employed what Anderson describes as "block shooting" to maximize her increasingly limited time and constant shape shifting. "We started block shooting my episodes. I would come in for three days at one point during the normal eight-day shooting schedule for an episode. We'd shoot all my appearances in an episode and then I would have some time off."

So seamless was the *X-Files'* creative teams' dealing with Anderson's pregnancy that her change of appearance was hardly noticeable in "Little Green Men" and "The Host," episodes that kicked off the second season. However, by the third episode,

"Blood," the keen-eyed *X-Files* aficionado could tell that Anderson was gradually fading into the background and that Mulder was, to a large extent, on his own. It was a fact not lost on David Duchovny in looking back on that period. "There was pressure," related the actor in a 1995 confabulation, "pressure to do better than we did in the first season. I saw the scripts coming in and I knew we'd be able to do it even with Gillian's absence."

Anderson, for her part, was amazed at how well her pregnancy was being handled by the rest of the cast and crew. "The writers were fantastic. There were so many things I could not do and so many things the camera could not do because there were only certain ways they could shoot me. But I felt everybody was doing a fabulous job given the limitations."

By her seventh month, Anderson was in the throes of the normal pregnant pauses—between-scene vomiting, severe mood swings, and physical changes that kept her in a constant state of shape shifting. But during one July day of filming, the actress, shifting uncomfortably in a chair, proved that, if nothing else, she had not lost her sense of humor. "I'm not a sex symbol," chuckles Anderson as she pats her belly. "I'm a reproduction symbol! This is easily the least sexy character I've ever played."

The creative contortions reached their apex with the much-touted back-to-back episodes "Duane Barry" and "Ascension," which chronicled Agent Scully's abduction and apparent delivery by the aforementioned mad agent into the hands of aliens for some outrageous experimentation. The tone of those shows was so over-the-top, even by *X-Files'* standards, that there was a real fear, despite sterling performances by Duchovny and stand-out guest performances by Steve Railsback and CCH Pounder, that in trying to save the show, Carter and company might have destroyed the very fiber of dark-and-light believability that held it together.

Anderson, in her last couple of months of the pregnancy, had by her own account "been limited to mostly sitting down or doing autopsy things." Typical of the series' way of doing things, Anderson's condition became the focal point of a bit of *X-Files* madness in this pivotal two-part story line.

With tongue firmly planted in cheek, Carter and company gave Anderson's pregnancy a fictional moment in the "Duane Barry" episode with a scene in which Scully is shopping in a supermarket and is shown purchasing pickles and ice cream. In "Ascension," Mulder has a fearful vision of Scully undergoing experimentation by unseen forces and, in particular, having her abdomen inflated to balloonlike proportions. For that sequence, Anderson willingly allowed her eight-month bulge to be photographed. "I'm not sure whose idea that was," recalls Anderson of her big belly scene. "But I have to admit I liked it."

This bit of trickery turned out to be the most outrageous example of a highly successful attempt to keep Anderson in the show. And no one was happier with the results than those who worked to make them happen. Producer Howard Gordon offers that Anderson's pregnancy was exactly the kind of thing that was needed to inject the series with a little bit of energy. Duchovny, in praising how *The X-Files* dealt with Anderson's pregnancy, is quick to point out that, despite the first season's critical success, the show had already fallen into a predictable and, often times, monotonous formula. "The monster-of-the-week episodes are fun," he declared in a 1996 interview, "but what makes the shows really great are the extended stories. I'm not sure we would have discovered those if Gillian had not gotten pregnant." Carter, when all was said and done, was equally satisfied. "I'm very pleased with the way the pregnancy added to the show rather than took away from it."

Anderson's pregnant pause in "Ascension" was her last official appearance on the show prior to delivering her baby. The one episode Anderson was totally absent from, titled "3," featured Duchovny solo in a tale of vampire love that guest-starred his then real-life girlfriend, actress Perrey Reeves.

Rumors spread like wildfire that "3" was an audition of sorts to determine whether Duchovny and Reeves could strike the same sparks on the tube as they apparently were doing in their love relationship. But "3" ultimately turned out to be a flat, lifeless, devoid-of-chemistry outing that pretty much drove home the point that the

Anderson-Duchovny chemistry was something that could not be duplicated.

In the meantime, as fall approached, Anderson was experiencing ups and downs with her emotional and physical well-being. When she had the strength to get out of her bed or chair, her steps were small and painfully awkward. Smiles from the normally radiant actress had become rare and rather forced. The regularly occurring kicks from inside her abdomen were sharp but welcome reminders. "When a woman gets pregnant she becomes, for a short period of time, a different person. Nothing felt familiar to me at that point. All I knew was that I was six times my normal size and that I had a baby kicking inside me in the middle of our doing scenes. I was happy. It had not been easy. But I was definitely ready to be a mother."

Anderson's gratitude to her supportive cast and crew is apparent. "They were always coming up to me on the set with encouraging words and there would be telephone calls. The positive support was important. Those were rough times and I don't know if I could have done it without them." Still, the stress of continuing to appear in *The X-Files*, even in her greatly reduced profile, was tremendous. So was the fact that her husband, because of the unpredictability of his freelance life, had largely been absent from the *X-Files* set, working on other, often out-of-town shows. There was also the fact that shortly after he and Gillian moved into a nondescript three-bedroom house in Vancouver following their wedding, the couple discovered themselves living in their own real-world X-File. "After my husband and I moved into our new house, I felt there were spirits there with us," she remembered in a 1995 conversation. "It was really creepy. It felt like there was someone attached to me. It was then that we were told by a local Native American that we were living near an Indian burial ground. We were told there had been a plague years ago in this area that had wiped many of them out and that there were a lot of souls in unrest. This person came to the house and performed a ritual in which herbs were burned to purify the space. It was amazing. Afterward it felt like the house got lighter and whatever we felt had been there was gone."

With the spirits of the dead now effectively out of the picture, the Anderson-Klotz house had more than enough room for their soon-to-be new arrival. Unfortunately, as the September 23 due date approached, doctors were finding indications that Anderson's delivery might not only be late but also entail an unconventional birth. No, it was not going to be the often-joked-about alien birth but rather a possible cesarean section that was being scheduled as a last-minute option should a normal delivery prove difficult. "The doctors discovered that the baby's head was too large and that it would not fit through my pelvis during a normal delivery," Anderson revealed in a 1996 conversation.

Anderson, two days after her projected due date, and only one day after completing her last day of *X-Files* duty, entered a Vancouver hospital and was prepped for a normal delivery. After she began what appeared to be normal labor, doctors discovered that the baby would not come out. The backup C-section was immediately implemented.

Gillian Anderson gave birth to an eight-pound ten-ounce baby girl on September

25, 1994. The baby was named Piper Anderson. The name, recalls Anderson, "came as the result of looking through my husband's old high school yearbook. We came across the name *Piper* and it just seemed to fit her personality so well. We knew right then that was the name."

Anderson, with her husband at her side, spent the next six days in the hospital and an additional four days at home in a "normal" recuperative state, which, for Anderson, entailed considerable pain. "I was up to my eyeballs in painkillers, Tylenol and things like that," she recalls. "And I was this real dreadful shade of blue after the operation."

Anderson had been counting on at least a month of recuperation time and Carter, at his most optimistic, was indicating to anyone who asked that "she would be allowed six weeks off to recover and spend some time at home." But six days after the birth of her daughter, the script for the next *X-Files* episode, titled "One Breath," showed up on her doorstep. "I had really been hoping for more time," said Anderson in a 1995 interview. "I was barely moving, I had just started to breast-feed, and I was still in a lot of pain. But the producers said 'you're in the next script,' and given all the changes I had put Chris and the show through, I felt it was my duty to go back when they wanted me. I definitely had postnatal depression, and I was finding it extremely hard to pull myself away from the baby physically. But I just had to go back to work."

Fortunately for Anderson, "One Breath," which finds Scully mysteriously showing up in a Washington hospital following her disappearance, has the actress in a comatose state for most of the episode. Less fortunate, in the same episode, was Scully's appearing equally out of it in a rowboat in the middle of a lake for a dream sequence.

Anderson returned to the set on October 5, 1994, still a little wobbly, occasionally off-balance, and with her daughter, Piper, and the baby's ever-present nanny. Of that episode, Anderson remembers very little that sounds pleasant. "People seemed really sorry for me. I was still quite blue from the operation, so I must have looked really awful, which seemed to perfectly fit the tone of the show. They put me out in the middle of this lake for about five hours, which was no picnic. I sat down as much as I could. I lay down as much as I could. I slept between scenes. I threw up between scenes."

According to the tabloids, Anderson was in so much pain after her return that she was supposedly bending over in pain during breaks in the filming of "One Breath." The actress, with more than a touch of sadistic glee, embellishes the tabloid tale. "I was breast-feeding and my breasts were real huge. I would have punctured them and fed everyone on the set. Can you imagine?"

Anderson has just returned to the set after a break during which she breast-fed Piper and was allowed the luxury of a few moments' rest. She walks, a bit unsteadily, across the soundstage to a hospital-room set and an estimated sixty or more cast and crew members hovering around. She stops, momentarily, to chat with the episode's director, R. W. Goodwin, who brings a laugh to Anderson at the suggestion that her lines have been unexpectedly changed. Wincing and in some obvious discomfort, Anderson eases herself into the bed. The scene about to be shot calls for Mulder to rage at the fate of his partner while Scully lies unmoving. At Goodwin's signal, Anderson closes her eyes. The scene unfolds with Mulder looking at Scully, finding himself helpless, and plotting revenge.

"Cut!" yells Goodwin.

Duchovny looks down at Anderson in the bed. Her eyes are still closed. He turns to face the crew, a big smile crossing his face. His finger comes up to his mouth in the classic quiet sign.

"She's asleep."

seven

I HEARD IT ON THE X

BUT NOT FOR LONG.

The next episode, "Firewalker," a good but not great episode involving scientists at a remote volcano where an unknown species of spore attaches itself to humans and bursts out of throats, was, following the complicated story arcs that preceded it, a relatively self-contained throwback to the style typical of the first season. The episode required a lot of physical action, including a sequence where Scully is dragged through the volcanic depths by a spore-infested scientist. Anderson, at that point, was admittedly not up to the task. "They hired a stunt double to do the more physical things for me," she recalls. "But that first episode back entailed a lot of running and jumping. It was physically difficult, and emotionally . . . well, I shed a lot of silent tears. It was horrible. There were plenty of times, during the first couple of episodes back, that all I wanted to do was quit and be with my baby. But, then, I would have had a lawsuit on my hands for breach of contract."

Anderson began to buck up emotionally in the episode titled "Red Museum," a truly creepy tale of a vegetarian cult in a town of beef producers. The presence of a full-time nanny helped. But, physically, she remembers that it was still touch and go. "Much as I'd like it to be, my body was not yet back in the shape it should be. Everything is a little off balance and not aligned yet. I know I have more weight to lose. And there's also a lot of motherly concerns. I'm still breast-feeding, and with a newborn, I'm not getting much rest. There's a general sense of exhaustion that's been following me around and I know the sleep deprivation is showing. I see the director of photography whispering to the makeup artist when they start applying makeup under my eyes, and I know what they're whispering about."

Anderson, however, found that she was able to put a lot of the mental and physical fatigue behind her in the wake of a writing staff that, seemingly, had gotten its second wind and was turning out truly excellent and, in emotional context, truly scary stories for the actress to deal with. One episode in particular, "Excelsis Dei," a tale of a ghostly presence at a nursing home which opens with a nurse being raped by the invisible entity, gave Anderson the shudders. "It was tough because it was a rape story. I was very aware of that element of the story. But it was also a good episode for my character in that Scully was more readily the believer in what was going on rather than in her usual role as total skeptic."

Anderson's emotional state came into play in the episode "Irresistible," a sick piece of business involving a death fetishist, which contained an equally powerful subplot with Scully suffering flashbacks to her abduction and, in a quite convincing manner, teetering precariously close to a complete breakdown. The final sequence in

"Irresistible" has Scully dissolving in tears. Carter relishes the emotional hoops he put Anderson through in this episode, which used the concept of denial as a driving point in the script. "We don't realize what the cumulative effect of emotional trauma can be on us and that sometimes it hits us in the weirdest places. I wanted this to hit Scully completely by surprise and force her to deal with a fear she does not know the cause of." Anderson recalls, "I had a scene in that episode in a psychiatrist's office, and it turned out to be a very good day to do it. I was very fortunate to be able to access and then suppress some stuff that was happening with me personally during that scene."

Anderson has always been vague about the "some stuff," but it is a known fact that she and her husband, who was working on other shows and occasionally out of town, were having some difficulties in the months following the birth of their daughter. And though she is noticeably uncomfortable with delving into the personal side of her life, she has left hints in recent conversations about those bumps in the road. "Right after Piper was born was a hard period for us," she laments. "Men don't have time during the pregnancy to connect with the child like the mother does. It was as if, suddenly, something came between the two of us and that there was this third person in the house. I can understand what Clyde was feeling. I was giving so much attention and love to this child. But one day it was no longer simply the mother and child with the father off to one side. It's a family."

Gavin Blair, an animated children's programming director who has worked with Klotz on his shows *Reboot* and *War Beast*, has had occasion to see the couple since the birth of their daughter and offers his impression. "They're pretty tight. Clyde's a pretty cool guy and he seems to be handling everything that is going on in his and Gillian's lives pretty well."

Anderson, with some prodding, also acknowledges that the stresses in their marriage have not all centered around the baby. "I'm very hard to be married to. Anybody in the situation I'm in right now would be hard to be married to. I'm incredibly strong willed. I want to do what I want to do."

As the second season progressed, it became evident to even the most casual observer that much of the tension surrounding *The X-Files* was not the sexual sparks, perceived or otherwise, between Mulder and Scully but rather to what degree Scully the Skeptic would be allowed to believe what was going on around her on a weekly basis. Carter acknowledges that Scully "has seen so much over the course of some forty-odd episodes" that for the character to continue to be totally unconvinced would "seem rather far-fetched."

But ongoing meetings between the producers and writers ultimately concluded that it was important to the balance of the show to keep Scully's skepticism and make it believable. A true test of that challenge emerged in the episode called "Fresh Bones," a tale of voodoo run amok in a resettlement camp for Haitian refugees. Though Scully falls victim to such voodoo hallucinations as a zombie materializing out of the palm of her hand, she manages to maintain her objective perspective.

Anderson remembers savoring her character's staunch skepticism in that episode.

"Growing up with a religious and military background, there is a kind of tightness and close-mindedness that has surrounded her life," she explains of her alter ego. "I think for someone to completely break away from a belief system and a way of thinking would take a long, long time."

It's 3 A.M. It's cold. It's raining. And Mulder and Scully are moving cautiously down the halls of an abandoned wing of a mental institution, guns drawn, about to come face to face with even more horrifying terrors than experienced in previous *X-Files* stories. *The X-Files* is having one of those kinds of nights. Take after take after take and no end in sight to what is shaping up as a long, sixteen-hour shoot. Piper's nanny, in a nearby trailer with the now six-month-old baby girl, is a bit spooked by it all and, at one point, is heard to exclaim, "I don't like it here. It's scary." Inside, the director has called "Cut! Let's try it again" for what seems like the hundredth time. Duchovny looks hangdog tired, his eyes glazed. Anderson is that and a whole lot more. It has been more than four hours since she's been able to break away and be with her daughter. She's anxious. Duchovny senses this and gives his costar an exaggerated shoulder massage. She smiles a tight smile.

The scene continues. Mulder and Scully cautiously round a darkened corner and discover a corpse lying on the floor in an advanced stage of decomposition. “Okay,” yells the director. “Let’s get the maggot wrangler in here.” A woman comes in carrying a jar. Inside the jar is a piece of raw liver. Crawling over the liver is a rather large colony of maggots. She bends over the form of the stuntman playing the corpse, opens the jar, and begins to pour the maggots over his body. Anderson and the rest of the crew, by this time really punchy, join in a resounding chorus of “Eecchh!” Duchovny screws up his face in squeamish disgust. The maggots begin to crawl all over the stuntman’s body and, at one point, one crawls over his eye. Anderson, more out of tired reflex than anything else, reaches over and nonchalantly plucks the maggot off his face and flicks it away. She shrugs and smiles sheepishly to a halfhearted round of applause.

Finally, the last shot of the night is in the can and the cast and crew are excused.

Anderson races to the trailer and takes Piper in her arms. Immediately her demeanor changes. She is bright and smiling, cooing baby talk at her daughter.

Anderson's maternal side appears quite natural. Longtime friend and director Gordon Edelstein remembers, "During the run of *The Philanthropist*, Gillian would sometimes come to my house for dinner. As soon as she would walk through the door, my youngest daughter would come running over to her, and they would get down on the floor and immediately be involved in some kind of game. You could tell by watching the two of them playing that Gillian would one day make a wonderful mother."

But what nobody, including Anderson herself, could have expected was the effect that having a child would ultimately have on her personality. Prior to becoming a mother, Anderson would regularly slip the likes of the Butthole Surfers and The Dead Kennedys into her CD player. Nowadays it doesn't get any heavier than Alanis Morissette, Emmylou Harris, or some traditional jazz or blues. "If I want to hear something really heavy, I'll put on the Foo Fighters or a good rocking Rolling

Stones song. That's about as intense as I get. I'm much milder than I was before." Even the subject matter of many *X-Files* episodes has kept her up nights. "There are lots of things in the show that have disturbed me, and I know that some of that comes from being a new mother. I'm suddenly hypersensitive to everything, and I used to be very fearless." She continues, "But I also felt that, after going through the birthing process, I was a much stronger person. I felt that no cut, no abrasion, and no knock on the head would ever make me whine again."

The second season of *The X-Files* continued to chug along. In the tension-packed "End Game," the second part of a two-part episode featuring a shape-shifting alien bounty hunter and the alleged return of Mulder's sister from years of apparent alien captivity, Scully is kidnapped by the alien before finally rescuing Mulder from certain icy death at the top of the world. In "Dod Kalm," Anderson and Duchovny had to endure four hours daily in the makeup chair for a story line that featured the agents aging while on a floating Bermuda Triangle. "It was a pain in the butt," recalls

Anderson of that experience, which featured, in a hilarious moment of outrage in a much-talked-about outtake, Anderson, in full old-age makeup, ending a line of dialogue by stating that "Howard Gordon [the episode writer] is a dead man."

Anderson and Duchovny had long complained about how the long hours and months required to do *The X-Files* allowed them little time for outside projects. But it was during the second season that Anderson made her first foray into outside work as the voice of a caricature named Data Nolly on the animated children's cartoon show *Reboot*. "Gillian and Clyde were big fans of the show, and word came to me that they would like to come down and take a look around our shop," remembers Gavin Blair, director of operations at the Canadian-based Main Frame Entertainment, the company that produced the show about two computer-generated characters. "While they were looking around, we mentioned to Gillian that we had always wanted to do a takeoff on *X-Files* and do a computer-generated version of Mulder and Scully. She was very enthusiastic about the idea and immediately agreed to do the voice."

The resulting episode of *Reboot*, titled "Trust No One," featured the caricatures of Fax Modem and Data Nolly hot on the heels of an energy vampire in Computer City and had Anderson zipping in and out of the Main Frame studios for a two-hour voice-over session for the episode, which aired early in 1996.

Anderson, unlike her *X-Files* alter ego, has always had a sense of childlike humor about her and, once the rigors of childbirth were over and she was back into her normal *X-Files* routine, that funny side began to reemerge. Once, during a marathon photo shoot that neither Anderson nor Duchovny was up to, the actress unexpectedly leaped into the arms of Duchovny, causing the normally introverted actor to break up in laughter. Fire extinguishers are also a favorite Gillian Anderson foil, and it was not uncommon during the second season for an unsuspecting crew member to walk by a desk only to have Anderson leap out from under it and let fly with the foamy spray. And a favorite ploy with directors, David Nutter and Rob Bowman in particular, is to have clothespin contests in which participants attach the pins to various parts of their bodies. Anderson, for the record, has a personal best of thirty-seven pins. "It happens all the time," chuckles Anderson. "Both David and I have mischievous streaks in us. When we mess up lines, it just ends up being funny. We just bust out laughing and we can't stop."

Anderson's humorous and somewhat demented side came into full play in "Humbug," in which Scully and Mulder stumble upon a town populated entirely by circus freaks. For the actress, it was just too good an opportunity to pass up. "Okay," says episode director Kim Manners. "Let's have the tattooed guy. Let's have the agents. Let's have the crickets." The scene in question is a relatively simple one, albeit bizarre in execution. Mulder and Scully, new in town, are seeking directions from a sideshow performer who is sitting inside a cauldron of water, chowing down on live crickets that are being poured in around him. The sequence called for Scully to reach in, pick out a specially designed chocolate cricket, and eat it. But a glint could be detected in Anderson's eyes. During one take, Anderson suddenly picks up one of the real crickets and, without missing a beat, calmly puts it in her mouth. Duchovny, known to cast and crew to be a bit on the squeamish side, makes a sour face and busts up, as do the director, the crew, and the tattooed guy. The actress, in perfect deadpan, has this reason for improvising. “I didn’t actually eat it. I put it in my mouth and then I spit it out. You’ve got to understand that I was there with this big guy. He’s sitting in this cauldron full of water, they pour this jar of crickets into his mouth, and he starts chomping on them. Now how can I justify putting my little hand in this jar and picking out just one to eat.”

The second season of *X-Files* continued to be a more chilling exercise, on average, than its predecessor, with episodes like “The Calusari,” “Soft Light,” and the nail-biting cliff-hanger “Anasazi” heightening the fear factor on a regular basis. Anderson, in these episodes, saw a gradual clearing up of some of her character’s deeper personal and professional agendas. “I think people are becoming intrigued by the relationship between Mulder and Scully, intrigued by the fact that there’s platonic professionalism and sexual tension at the same time. I think the relationship with Scully and Mulder has changed. They're more easygoing and comfortable with each other, and I think that has come about because of everything they've been through together. They've gone through so much and have risked their lives for each other so many times that they've developed this intense, thick, unspoken bond between them." She elaborates, "But, despite the fact that Scully has had moments where she's seen Mulder's side of things, I've liked the idea that she hasn't become a true believer. Even though Scully has experienced a lot, her background continues to be ingrained in science and medicine. That's where her mind goes first in terms of solving the mysteries that Scully and Mulder come up against. Scully is as open as she's going to get."

The show's second season officially ended on May 11, 1995. Anderson could, for a short time at least, devote her energies to being a wife and mother. And it is a period that the actress relishes because she is admittedly having a rough emotional time keeping all the balls in the air. "The show has forced me to focus and become much more responsible and make much healthier choices because there's a responsibility that I have to myself, the show, and the family. In the last department I've been particularly blessed. Piper keeps me in check, and my husband has kept me quite grounded." She continues with her usual candor, "I have had the best days and the worst days of my entire life over the past year. Yes, I am beat and, yes, there have been times when I thought all of this was just too much. But having Piper has taken a lot of the focus off of me and has put it on something that is much more important. . . . This time has been very frustrating for me. I'm finding that I'm not taking the work as seriously as I have taken it in the past. I'm still putting as much energy as I can into the show, but I'm just not as obsessed with it as I was before. I feel like I owe it to the people I work with to be professional, but I won't lie and say it hasn't been hard for me."

In a moment of self-reflection, Anderson succinctly sums up the many changes she's undergone in the past couple years. "What has finally caught up with me is basically the facts of my life." And it is those facts that put her real life at odds with Dana Scully's concept of reality. "Scully is so serious," sighs Anderson. "She's way too smart for anybody's good. There is nothing that this woman doesn't know. And she's so damned career minded. I don't think she would understand my life. Scully would probably think my life is a little weird."

eight

GILLIAN UNCHAINED

EVERY TIME GILLIAN ANDERSON TURNED AROUND she saw David Duchovny. No, it was not on the set of *The X-Files* or in her dreams. It was in the guest seat on late-night talk shows and on the covers of national magazines. In the race for publicity, Duchovny was way out ahead.

One reason for Anderson's relatively low profile may rest with her less-than-manic pursuit of publicity early in the show's existence. "I don't think I've found fame yet," she explained as recently as 1995. "It's found me, but I don't think I've found it. Fame, at the moment, feels like a lot of hard work. I get a few tastes of what fame is supposed to be. The only time I get to participate in it is when we do something like an awards ceremony and everybody's there."

In all fairness, Anderson has been the victim of inexperience and bad timing when it's come to dealing with the media. Prior to landing her role in *The X-Files*, the actress had done only one press interview in the early 1990s, with the *New York Times* in conjunction with *Absent Friends*. Understandably, she was a little shy and withdrawn in those early contacts. And, unlike Duchovny, who had a solid background and a ragged upbringing to exploit, Anderson's limited and obscure career, coupled with a reluctance to talk about the more controversial aspects of her life, resulted in rather bland early press that concentrated primarily on her character and the show.

The actress, looking back on that period, offers that a big part of her radically skewed early press coverage may have had a lot to do with people in the media not being inclined to look too deeply. "People tend to think I'm conservative because of the character I play on the show. Because of Scully, they treat me like I'm a very nice person. And they're not wrong, because I do think I'm a nice person. But they seem to have a hard time taking some other things in. . . . I have a tendency to ramble, and I'm not very good at sound bites, so often magazines end up writing about me from their own point of view. They'll put in a few short quotes from me, and invariably they'll end up being the most uninteresting. I'm goofy and I say a lot of goofy, silly things, and few of the stories I read about me have captured that side of my personality."

Anderson slowly but surely became more press savvy, but by that time she had become pregnant and, consequently, was doing a lot of "Yes, I'm pregnant. How will it affect the show?" interviews that, though not necessarily casting her in a negative light, seemed to pigeonhole her as the show's resident loose cannon. Adding insult to injury, it was during her much-publicized pregnancy that Duchovny's press profile hit an all-time high, with the actor's mug appearing on the cover of magazines like *Entertainment Weekly* and in the coveted seat on *The Tonight Show* stage. "He was getting all the covers," recalls *For Him Magazine* feature editor Anthony Noguera, "and she was getting nothing. She was being sidelined away."

Anderson, initially slow to anger on the publicity issue, began to grouse about the seeming inequity. "It's odd how even though most of the time we're both in every scene and we work as partners together, the show is being billed and promoted as being about Mulder," she recalled in a 1995 conversation. "And a lot of the scripts are centered around his struggles and his beliefs, whether Scully ends up solving the case or not. It's frustrating sometimes because I feel I'm working just as hard." And as recently as 1996, when Anderson had finally risen to fan and press favorite on a par with her costar, there was still a touch of resentment. "At first I felt like, this is our show. It wasn't just his show. But I've learned not to care so much."

But Anderson definitely cared when, following the completion of the second season, she was whisked off to Europe to begin publicizing the premiere of *The X-Files* on the European continent. This time things would be a lot different. Whereas Anderson and Duchovny were joined at the hip during press outings during the first two seasons, Anderson was on her own this time. She was also faced with a European press that, unlike the mainstream and science-fiction press in the States, was much more interested in probing into aspects of her personal life and attitudes.

Rather than cringe at the prospect of dealing with hard questions, Anderson, perhaps feeling a kinship to Europe and its more progressive ways, seemed to respond with a renewed confidence, going into some detail about areas of her life that she had either glossed over or flat-out refused to talk about a year earlier. It was during this round of press coverage that the first fragmented looks into Anderson's troubled childhood came to light. And, though she never divulged his name, Anderson began to admit that, yes, she had gone from New York to Los Angeles to be with her lover.

Overall, Anderson may not have been revealing anything particularly earth-shaking, but the European trip did serve to make her more forthcoming, and consequently the interest sparked by the latest round of press made her more in demand when she returned to Vancouver in the late summer of 1995 in preparation for the start of *The X-Files'* third season.

Anderson's newfound ease with the press could not have come at a better time. *The X-Files* was no longer a cult show but rather a series that had made major strides into the mainstream world of television. The flood of merchandise—the comic books and novels, *Mad* magazine's parody "The Ecch Files," the T-shirts and coffee mugs and, yes, even an *X-Files* porno movie, *The XXX Files*, that featured the erotic adventures of Boulder and Skulky (as played by porn actress Tyffany Million)—had made its way into the marketplace. "I don't think it's hit me yet just how popular this show has become," says Anderson. "I did think that, when we started on season two, this thing might be going on for a while. I think, at that point, we all had the feeling that we might be caught up in this for the long haul."

Anderson, during her European jaunt, was adamant in stating her feelings that a third-season character change for Scully was in order. "I think Scully has been chasing in Mulder's footsteps long enough. They've certainly written her as competent enough to do the investigations, and it gets tiring to always have this character being one step behind. At first it made sense because Scully had not witnessed very much, but I think now that she has, it's time to move forward with her. The first season was about finding our way with the show. The second season was about the pregnancy. Now I think it's time for Mulder and Scully to be equal partners."

The Anderson-Duchovny pair also became business partners of a kind during the hiatus. Both actors had asked for and received an increase in pay, reportedly to the tune of $100,000 per episode for Duchovny and, grouses Anderson, "I'm now making a little more than half of what David makes," and the perk of having to do two fewer episodes per season for the remaining lifetime of the show.

The two-episode season opener, "The Blessing Way" and "Paper Clip," immediately put Scully in conspiracy hell. While Mulder is fighting for his life as the result of the events that took place in the previous season's cliff-hanger, Scully embarks on a solo investigation that puts her at odds with Cancer Man and ultimately leaves her emotionally distraught when events conspire to keep her from being at the bedside of her dying sister who was shot by a mysterious assassin who mistook her for Scully.

The X-Files took an unexpected turn at that point, putting the alien conspiracy story line on hold in favor of a series of stories focusing on madmen and serial-killer types that, much like the first season, centered on linear storytelling and offered Anderson little to chew on beyond the tried-and-true Scully stance. "Syzygy," a passable stab at the teens-with-psychic-powers subgenre, is notable for its hilarious moment when Mulder, under the influence of the teens, is discovered by Scully about to do the deed with an equally possessed police detective. Anderson's reaction and some quibbling banter between Mulder and Scully are the high points.

The return to aliens and government coverups comes with the two-parter "Nisei" and "731," in which the murder of the vendor of an alien autopsy video sets off an action-packed series of events and intrigues. Anderson is finally given some beef as she has flashbacks of her alien abduction and follows up clues to possible government alien-human hybrid experiments. The episode that follows, the bug invasion of "War of the Coprophages," allows some comedic opportunities for Scully to be marginally jealous of Mulder's purely professional involvement with Bambi the entomologist. Anderson offers that the episode, which has both defenders and detractors, gave viewers some insight into the dark recesses of the Mulder-Scully relationship. "I think that because of how intimately and intensely Mulder and Scully work together, that anytime there's anybody that comes up around the other, it causes a little bit of tension. Needless to say, Bambi caused a little bit of tension."

Gillian Anderson looks out the window of her plane as Los Angeles looms up ahead. Her plane circles in for its final approach to LAX. In her mind, Anderson was taking a big chance.

X-Files conventions had become a natural outgrowth of the popularity of the show, and so it was inevitable that offers, financially lucrative offers at that, would come pouring in to the cast and creators of the show to appear in the flesh, answer a few questions, and sign a few autographs. Chris Carter, despite his maddening schedule, had been quick to climb on the convention train. In due time Mitch Pileggi, Steven Williams, and every second-line regular and guest star worth their salt were making appearances. In fact, the only two who had continued to say thanks but no thanks were Duchovny and Anderson. The odds are that Duchovny will never do one and that it will cost somebody an arm and a leg if he does. Anderson, however, had a higher level of curiosity and just had to experience one to see what it was all about.

The plane taxied to a stop in front of the terminal and the passengers got off. Anderson walked down the gangway and into the brightly lit terminal, where she was met by four polite and massive security types who had been hired by the convention to protect their prize package. Anderson recalls that the four men immediately surrounded her, forming a shield around her. "I was walking with my arms folded right in the middle of these people. It was the most bizarre thing in the world."

Anderson was driven by limo to the

famed Four Seasons hotel, where she spent the three days prior to the convention doing scattered press interviews and, rumor has it, inquiring into possible film roles during the next hiatus. Mostly, however, she spent her time being reminded, in a most uncomfortable manner, that she has become something special that must be protected.

Anderson spends a sleepless night before the convention, tossing and turning as she thinks about her husband and child and suffers a bad case of preconvention nerves. Her security is never far away, a fact that both astounds and dismays her. While eating a meal in the hotel restaurant on the day of the convention, she is approached by one of her security guards, who reports in polite, even tones, "Everything is clear. When you come out, I'll be there." Anderson looks after him as he leaves, and other heads in the restaurant turn to follow him as well. She sighs and finishes her meal. She's barely past the cash register when her protectors materialize around her and escort her through the lobby to the front of the hotel, where a long, white stretch limo waits. Anderson, visibly upset, looks from her security to the limo, back to the security, and finally back to the limo. "This is just too much!"

Anderson, for all her trepidation about doing the convention, ended up having a rather pleasant time. The question-and-answer session was a mixture of extreme fan gushing, questions she's heard a hundred times, and a handful of personal inquiries that she found easy to deflect or gloss over. Gillian, after the convention appearance, insisted that this was her first and last attempt to meet her fans on this public a level. But she also made no bones about the fact that the experience had been a pleasant one. "Everybody was normal," chuckles Anderson in reference to the fact that convention types are often pegged as obsessed no-lifes. "I thought that everybody was going to be really, really strange and that they would shake and have three noses. But it wasn't like that at all."

Success, it is safe to say, has not made life on the *X-Files* set any easier. It's still long days and nights in often unforgiving weather. But for Anderson, doing the episode titled "The Pusher" had some side distractions. Present on the set was *For Him Magazine* features editor Anthony Noguera. Now, having reporters hanging around the set asking Gillian questions was nothing new. But this men's magazine, known for its offbeat approach to dealing with celebrities, was after something different in its quest for Gillian Anderson. "We think Gillian Anderson is sexy, and we think she can be interesting," says Noguera. "But we've never read anything interesting about her. All the interviews have been fairly bland and they've treated her like she was Dana Scully. We wanted to know what she was like as a person, and we did not want to talk about Dana Scully or *The X-Files* to any great degree."

Adding to the journalistic tension is that in between moments of conversation with Noguera, Anderson must slip in and out of her Dana Scully persona for a nerve-racking scene in which a brain tumor patient with the power to influence people has forced Mulder into a game of Russian roulette that is interrupted by Scully's arrival.

Veteran *X-Files* director Rob Bowman has just come in from the near zero temperature and is in a discussion with his director of photography for the latest element of this scene. Duchovny is off in a corner of the set, taking deep breaths, slumping his shoulders, and getting very much into the moment. At another corner of the set, this episode's guest, Robert Wisden, is looking slightly demonic as a fresh coat of makeup is applied. Anderson arrives on the set and takes off her coat to reveal her regulation FBI duds, supplemented by a bullet-proof vest. Anderson goes to her mark.

At Bowman's signal, Scully bursts into the room. "You bastard! Damn you! Damn you!" The mind monster immediately forces Mulder to point the gun at Scully and fire. Scully dives for cover and ends up crashing into a wall.

"Cut!" yells Bowman. "Now let's do it again."

This kind of grueling exercise is par for the course. What is not is that the normally reserved Anderson, through the skillful interviewing of Noguera, is giving up secrets of her troubled youth, tales of sexual and alcohol excess, without batting an eye. "Gillian was very nervous," recounts the reporter of that interview. "I think she found it strange that we wanted to talk to her. No one had ever approached her before as a person, and she had never been asked some of the questions that I asked her. People for the most part are afraid to ask celebrities normal questions, what they believe in, what turns them on, what makes them laugh. I think Gillian found it quite attractive that we were going to treat her like a person."

A nondescript limo pulls to a stop in front of a secluded photo studio in the wilds of Hollywood. Anderson and a small entourage emerge and walk into the studio. After greeting the photographer and his staff, the actress is led to an adjacent wardrobe room where the clothes she will wear for the magazine shoot are laid out. Anderson looks at the clothes. A very un-Scully low-cut, black lacy thing. Something equally tight and black. A cat suit. A man's shirt. Anderson's eyes grow wide and she laughs. A little girl's laugh.

Not only is *For Him Magazine* intent on portraying Anderson as a real person but also on putting a sexual fantasy spin on the perceived straitlaced Scully image. Anderson, perhaps surprisingly, readily agreed to the photo session, but now as she walks out into the studio in the black, low-cut, formfitting dress, she is a little self-conscious. "I've got a big butt," she mutters to nobody in particular. She smiles when those around her say she looks great, which, in her understated makeup and hairstyle, she does.

The course of the photo shoot runs the gamut from the ridiculous (Anderson in the cat suit perched on a ledge forty feet in the air) to the sublime (Anderson in the black lace nightwear in various reclining poses on a bed). As the session progresses, Anderson begins to get more comfortable with her altered state. While in the lingerie, she jokes with the photographer that her C-section scar is too low down to be seen. And, in a very Anderson but not very Scully moment, she laughingly agrees with a joking notion that she should be tied to the bed for a series of photos. "Great!" chuckles Anderson. "Where do we start?"

Watching Anderson primp, pout, and strike various sultry poses during the course of the day reveals that the actress with the straitlaced reputation is warming to the idea of being, even for a few moments, a sex goddess. As the shoot draws to a close, a photographer's assistant allows that nobody is going to believe this is Agent Scully. Anderson responds, "That's the point."

After the photo shoot, the actress hopped a plane and immediately returned to Vancouver to be on the set the following Monday for the start of the next episode, "Teso Dos Bichos." Anderson took some good-natured ribbing from those who were privy to where she had been, but that was the least of her problems. This new episode, which chronicles the exploits of a cursed South American relic taking revenge on those who have disturbed its sleep, required Mulder and Scully, at one point, to come in close contact with an army of killer cats. Anderson is allergic to cats. Enter some quick-thinking special-effects people who, for the extreme close-ups of Scully battling the cats, rigged cat dummies covered with rabbit fur. "It was the stupidest thing I've ever done," winces Anderson at the memory. "It was take after take of rolling around with this bunny-covered cat on my face. The fur was coming off, going up my nose, and sticking to my lipstick. That was absolutely the worst."

It was a couple of months later when the much-anticipated *For Him Magazine* article came out. The cover photo caption, "Gillian Anderson X-Rated! Undercover with Agent Scully," over a provocative shot of Anderson in cleavage-revealing black lace, hair down, and a come-hither look in her eyes, was an immediate sensation. So was the inside photo spread and the intimate interview on the inside pages. The effect when the magazine hit the stands was immediate and predictable. A small percentage of fans, who obviously take *The X-Files* a little too seriously, were outraged that their virginal image of Dana Scully had been dashed. One irate Internet surfer posted a message claiming that the interview had either been made up or that Anderson was a bimbo and an airhead. But Anderson herself seemed pleased. "I think she was possibly a little surprised," said Noguera. "She had never seen herself in this way. But she liked it. She thought it was fun."

The article was also the catalyst to catapult Gillian Anderson into the media stratosphere. The phone began ringing off the hook. The world had suddenly discovered that there was more to Gillian Anderson than Agent Dana Scully. "She's a very down to earth, approachable person," reflects Noguera. "She's a very famous woman, but she is a woman. Scully doesn't swear. Gillian Anderson does."

Anderson, warming to the press attention, recalls that on her recent trip to Los Angeles she was pleasantly surprised to discover a copy of *TV Guide* with Duchovny and her on the cover. "It's pretty neat, but at the same time there are so many magazines out there that we have not been a part of, and that's always on my mind."

TV Guide was the first outlet to effectively capitalize on the new frontier opened by *For Him Magazine*. Having already featured *The X-Files* on their cover three previous times, all with Duchovny and Anderson sharing the space, the magazine offered Anderson a solo cover and a 1940s fashion-oriented photo layout. In addition, they were willing to come to Vancouver to do the agreed-upon one-day photo shoot and interview.

The photo shoot, taking place in a hotel room not too far from the *X-Files* studio, has Anderson posing in various reclining and sitting positions on a bed in such costumes as a gold dress with plunging neckline, a sleek black suit with a veil, a silk dressing gown with feathers, and four-inch heels. "It's fun to dress up," says Anderson during the day. "But I wouldn't want to do it all the time. There's something to be said for putting on a nice dress and getting all glammed up. But that's not who my character is."

TV Guide's attempts at making Anderson a Vargas pinup come to life prove a lot less stressful than her photo shoot initiation with *For Him Magazine*—so much, in fact, that the session is regularly interrupted by Anderson erupting into giggling fits. It happens when she stumbles while trying to balance herself on her heels. It happens again when the feathers come loose and tickle her face. The photographer, who initially goes along with the laughs, is getting a little impatient. Finally, he gives up and brings the session to a halt for the day.

TV Guide's article turned out to be a

PG-rated version of the story in *For Him Magazine*, with Anderson giving up few details and giving her patented glossed-over answers to the more personal questions. But given the giddy nature of the photo session, the photos make a more elegant, classy statement compared with the racy photos in *For Him Magazine*.

Anderson, along with Duchovny and *X-Files* creator Carter, had one more shot at the media's sudden interest in the fantasy potential of *The X-Files* in 1996, when *Rolling Stone* invaded the show's Vancouver turf for a cover story on the popularity of the show. The story, which featured a question-and-answer format with Anderson, Duchovny, and Carter, shed little if any new light on the show or the actors. But, oh, that cover! Everybody's fantasy of Anderson and Duchovny in bed together, looking very naked and embracing in that oh-so-special way. Anderson, at the time, had a good laugh at the experience, exclaiming, with tongue firmly planted in cheek, "It was good for me."

In fact, the fantasy cover was such a kick for Anderson that months later when a reporter asked about the feasibility of a

Scully-Mulder romance, she imaginatively responded, "It would be great to eventually see them have the greatest sex in the world, just as a relief for the whole audience as well as for them. We could have an entire hour devoted to just Mulder and Scully in bed together. We could have a half hour of foreplay and then raunchy sex with everything from handcuffs to chandeliers over our heads. In fact that could be the *X-Files* movie everybody has been talking about. Just Scully and Mulder and a bed."

The remainder of the *X-Files'* third season turned out to be a mix of opportunities for Anderson and her character. In the episode "José Chung's 'From Outer Space'" Scully is portrayed in a maddeningly stolid stance as she interviews alien abduction writer José Chung. But easily the most powerful moment during the show's third season could be seen in *X-Files'* homage to the Loch Ness monster in "Quagmire." The episode, which follows Mulder and Scully to an isolated lake where mysterious mutilation killings have been attributed to the lake's legendary denizen, Big Blue, is a fairly subpar bit of foolishness until the third act, when the two agents, trapped on a tiny island while the monster lurks somewhere in the fog-shrouded water, engage in a hauntingly personal conversation that questions just what their relationship to each other is. It is a sequence so powerful that when Big Blue actually makes an appearance at the fade, it pales in comparison.

Anderson, whose life a year earlier was in personal and professional turmoil, readily admits that she feels as though she's survived the trials by *X-Files* that have turned her life upside down. "There have been numerous times when I thought that all this was going to break me," she reflected in a 1996 interview. "But it hasn't and now I feel stronger about everything than I have."

nine

MOONLIGHTING

Gillian Anderson has never made any bones about the fact that *The X-Files* would not be the beginning and the end of her career. The actress has indicated on several occasions that producing is on her wish list "because of its hands-on creative aspects." Writing and directing, on the other hand, owing to the inherent stress level, are not up quite as high. And no, Anderson is not quick to put aside acting. In fact, the opposite seems to be the case. "I don't want to do a movie of the week," Anderson related during a 1994 conversation when questioned about what she plans for her free time. "My fantasy right now is a small role in a feature film. Obviously the script would be what's important. It would be important that the character be very different from Scully because I want the audience to see that I can do something else."

Consequently, when *The X-Files* wrapped up its third season with the white-knuckle cliff-hanger "Talitha Cumi," Anderson, with Piper at eighteen months more travel friendly, set her sights on making the most of her hiatus. Immediately the rumors of movie roles began to fly, fueled to some extent by Anderson herself, who indicated during an interview in 1995 that she was considering "a part in a movie with Morgan Freeman and a part in a giant snake movie called *Anaconda*." But neither of these or any other film offers actually came to fruition.

Buoyed by the response to her voiceover work in *Reboot*, Anderson did agree to do the voiceover work for a one-hour pseudo-documentary called *Why Planes Go Down*, which, with the aid of filmed footage and news accounts, explored the phenomenon of plane crashes.

Why Anderson chose this particular

project remains a bit of a mystery. Because the show was a Fox network project, one would guess that there was some subtle pressure put on Anderson to ensure a ratings success. And the money had to have been real good. But Anderson, or her handlers, must have had an inkling, too, that this was something more quick buck than class act.

Why Planes Go Down aired in April 1996. Predictably, Anderson's much-publicized off-screen work on the special hooked the *X-Files* audience, and the ratings were respectable. Critically, however, the show's exploitative tabloid approach took a beating, as did, in many reviews, Anderson herself. In an April 22, 1996, *New York Times* review of the special, Walter Goodman wrote, "Anderson delivers her script as though it were a public service announcement for visitors to Hades. What she ought to be offering is coffee, scotch, or Prozac."

Midway through the third season, Anderson, Duchovny, and Carter struck a deal with Fox Interactive to do a live-action CD-ROM game with the working title of "25th Season: 3 Episode." Anderson and Duchovny shot footage specifically for the game toward the end of the third season. Though the story line for the *X-Files* game, due for release sometime in 1997, is top secret, what is known is that the game will allow players to interact with the two characters, deal with witnesses and clues, and ultimately solve an *X-Files*-style mystery.

Though anxious to do outside work, Anderson continued to be cautious. "When I first started doing *X-Files*, I was inundated by requests to do anything and everything to do with science fiction and the paranormal, but I turned it all down. A lot of what I was being offered was not real intelligent and seemed to be more than just a little bit exploitive." But a trip to England during this period to promote *The X-Files* resulted in a job offer that was right up her alley, an on-screen hosting chore for the nine-part BBC science-fiction/science-fact series called *Future Fantastic*. The series explores the relationship between science fiction and science fact, and with a focus on how imagination can lead to scientific reality, it examines such topics as robots, time travel, and aliens.

Series director David McNab recalls that Anderson was contacted about narrating *Future Fantastic* in March 1996. "Gillian's agent made it very plain that she had been offered a lot of these kinds of things lately," recalls the director, "but we went ahead and submitted the treatments for the show and hoped for the best."

McNab and company got the best when Anderson enthusiastically jumped at the chance to be involved in something that she perceived to be a highbrow adjunct to what she had been doing on *The X-Files*. "I think she went for it for a couple of reasons," speculates McNab. "One was that it was a BBC production and, having grown up in England, she had a real affinity for something being done in a country that was, essentially, her second home. And, although the show was about science fiction and included stuff about aliens, robots, and time travel, it came from a scientific base that had some respectability. She had decided, in her words, that it was not a flaky series."

Anderson, with Piper in tow, flew to New York, where the first two days of a four-day shooting schedule were to begin (the last two days would be shot in Los Angeles). It was hot in New York and the days would be long, so the day before she began filming, Anderson put Piper on a plane back to Vancouver. It was one of those small moments that tugged at her equally strong professional and maternal sides. In addition, the actress was tentative during the first day of filming the series links on the top floor of a warehouse near the waterfront. "It was terribly hot that first day," reflects McNab, "and so it was incredibly draining. Gillian was weary and frazzled and was probably missing Piper just a bit." But the director remembers that Anderson quickly warmed to the occasion. "After that [first] day she loosened up and was terrific fun. She would join in the crew jokes and really got into the spirit of things. By the end of the fourth day, she was really one of the team."

Anderson's professionalism during these sessions was obvious. She was quick, which in narration work is an immediate plus. "She is easily one of the brightest people I've ever worked with. She has no scientific training, but she was continuously questioning not only the way things were written but whether the stuff she was saying was actually true. She also came up with some quite valid suggestions for rewriting parts of the script that would make a lot more sense," remarked McNab. "I'm really excited about presenting this show," enthuses Anderson. "The subjects of this show could very easily have come out of *X-Files*. But this show proves that science fiction is often the inspiration behind science fact and reveals that anything we can imagine is possible somewhere, somehow."

Anderson's distinctive voice, sexy, detached, and cool, was quickly making her a hot property in the world of documentary narration. Although she still had her sights set on the big screen, her interest in supporting educational and documentary programs was pricked when the production team of Martha Ostertag and Kurt Sayenga came calling in November 1995 with *Spies Above*. The film, which aired early in 1996 on the Discovery Channel and is currently available in video stores, tells the history of satellite photographic espionage from its inception in a very dark wing of the Eisenhower administration to its current status in the 1990s.

"Kurt and I are both big fans of women narrators," says Ostertag, "especially when the topic concerns government-type classified topics. Given that, we felt Gillian would be absolutely perfect to do this film. She was our first and only choice, but her role in *X-Files* did make her the perfect person to do it." Sayenga offers, "I was very much into the punk rock scene, and I knew that Gillian had a background in that scene, which made me inclined toward using her. And being an ardent fan of *X-Files* I immediately began playing with the notion of trying to get her. The timing seemed to be good. *X-Files* was about to break out of cult status into mainstream popularity, and there had not been a big publicity push behind Gillian yet. So we actually felt that we had a chance of getting her."

Ostertag chuckles as she explains that the Discovery Channel, amazingly enough, "did not have a clue as to why we wanted to use her. Obviously they were of a generation that was not familiar with *X-Files*. But basically everybody aged forty or under said 'My god! Of course!'"

Then it was simply a matter of getting Anderson to say yes to the project. Sayenga recalls producer Ostertag approaching Anderson's people late in 1995 as the third season of *The X-Files* was winding down. "She was inclined to do it," he remembers. "At that point people were getting hip to the fact that she had this fantastic voice that was perfect for documentaries and had been approached by a number of entities. What happened was Gillian looked at a number of projects and said ours sounded the coolest."

Ostertag, Sayenga, and their crew flew to Vancouver on a Saturday night in mid-December 1995 and set up shop in the same soundstage where Anderson does her voiceovers for *The X-Files*. Sayenga, who had been rewriting portions of the script on the plane and in his hotel, called Anderson immediately. Anderson, with Piper crying in the background, picked up the phone. "Gillian was really intent on getting the script ahead of time and figuring it out," relates the director-writer. "It was a tough script that talked about a lot of complex things, and she wanted to make sure she would sound like she knew what she was talking about."

Anderson's truck pulled into the parking lot of Pinewood Studios on a Sunday night about 6 P.M. The actress, clearly exhausted from the combination of *The X-Files* and motherhood, entered the studio and was greeted by Sayenga, who was all set up and ready to go. "I was immediately struck by the fact that she was much prettier in person than she was on television," he remembers. "I mean she looks nice on television, but she looks fantastic in real life. She definitely dresses much cooler than Scully does."

Unfortunately, Sayenga also immediately noticed that Anderson was sniffling and sneezing. "She had a cold, which was not what you want to hear when you're going into a narration session. Postponing at that point was not an option. We had to get it done, and I had to rush the tape back almost immediately."

Anderson moved to the recording booth and, with a modicum of small talk, opened her script to page one. Sayenga's original intent was to have Anderson read her script to the already assembled documentary. But her illness was making a true reading, under those conditions, impossible. "It was going slowly," he says of the session. "We got about a tenth of the way through the script and we both realized that reading to the picture was not an option. At the rate we were going it would have taken two days, and neither one of us had that kind of time."

It was decided that Anderson would just read the script through. Anderson, at one point, stepped out for a cigarette but otherwise breezed through the script, with an occasional pause to crack a joke with Sayenga, in a matter of hours. For the director, the reading was everything he had imagined. "She gave it that nice, super-serious, deadpan delivery that I wanted. In a sense it was almost like having Scully reading it, which really made it perfect."

Anderson left the studio at 10 P.M., and Sayenga returned to the States to put the finishing touches onto *Spies Above*. Shortly thereafter he turned the completed documentary in to the Discovery Channel. "And some of the people at Discovery just didn't get it," recalls Sayenga about what happened next. "They were not sure about Gillian and wanted to replace her with a traditional male narrator. We were finished, but there was suddenly a definite possibility that she would be replaced. I hit the ceiling. Ultimately, the people who weren't sure about Gillian were convinced that it had been obvious from the beginning that having Gillian Anderson narrate a story about spy satellites was a good idea.”

The folks at Microsoft felt that having Gillian Anderson do the voice of a computer named E.V.E. in the CD-ROM combat game Hellbender was also a good idea. Anderson knocked out the various possibilities for Hellbender in a day. Anderson’s CD-ROM debut was scheduled for a 1997 release.

Also during this period, Anderson and Duchovny closed a deal with the producers of *The Simpsons* for yet another voice-over adventure in an episode called “The Springfield Files,”* in which Mulder and Scully come to town to investigate Homer Simpson’s alien encounter. The show aired to critical acclaim and fantastic ratings in January 1997.

Anderson’s time away from *The X-Files* was not all work, however. During a short publicity jaunt to Milan, Italy, to promote the show, Anderson, with her mother, daughter, and husband along, spent some quiet time taking in the Italian sights. Then she returned to Vancouver, where she spent a lot of time around the house, playing with her daughter. She giggles, "At least once a week I would lay back in the bathtub and just laugh at the ridiculousness of it all."

Ridiculous has definitely become the watchword as the press has discovered that a lot of papers and magazines can be sold if Gillian Anderson is somewhere in their pages. Although the rush of paparazzi is an annoyance that Anderson, for the most part, has been able to deal with, her notoriety has caused her to change her habits. Whereas she was once quite comfortable walking down the streets of Vancouver and other major cities when *The X-Files* was still a cult item, she now regularly makes use of security systems and back entrances. And her look is less than cheerful when somebody attempts to take a picture of Piper. Her parents and old school chums have also made an informal pact to protect Gillian's privacy at all costs. But, according to Anderson's mother, Rosemary, that has not stopped members of the British tabloid press from invading Anderson's home town of Grand Rapids in May of 1996. "This reporter showed up at my front door in the pouring rain," explained Rosemary Anderson. "My girlfriend was in the driveway, and she practically pushed her out of the way. She said, 'I'm from London and I'd like to interview you about Gillian Anderson and her childhood and have some pictures and use some of your time.' In fact she's still in town now, holed up in a hotel, calling just about everybody in town we've ever known. She's been over to the high school and has gone through yearbooks. God knows what she's found!"

Anderson, during the hiatus, continued to rack up frequent flyer miles between Vancouver and Los Angeles and New York for the purpose of raising her already-in-the-stratosphere profile with photo shoots, meetings, and interviews. While still secretive about future work, she does indicate, during this period, that her feelings about doing the long-rumored *X-Files* movie have begun to waver. "Nobody's ever really formally approached me about doing it," she claimed during a 1996 conversation. "At this point I have tentative plans to do one or two different films next year separate from *The X-Files*, so hopefully they'll come to me before I make any plans. If not, too bad, because I won't be part of it."

ten

AND THE WINNER IS . . .

The sun was just starting to break over the soundstages of Vancouver's North Shores Studios. It would be at least three hours before Gillian Anderson drove into the parking lot. But the first signs of life on the fourth season of *The X-Files* were already in evidence. Production designers were hard at work, touching up the standing sets of Walter Skinner's office and Mulder's apartment, adding the necessary props required for the season's opening episode, titled "Herrenvolk." Scripts were being read over, with lines of dialogue edited and camera angles revised in thick pencil strokes.

David Duchovny pulls into the parking lot, fresh from a quick stopover in New York to see his mother and friends. He opens the car door, and Blue, his faithful dog, jumps out and proceeds to run around the grounds, marking his territory. Anderson, with Piper and the ubiquitous nanny in tow, arrives shortly afterward. Piper, nearly three years old, walks hand in hand with Anderson to her trailer.

"I consider myself very lucky to be able to bring Piper to work with me every day," Anderson declares. "Piper has a very wild personality and so she's quite adaptable to all the wild things that go on on the set of this show everyday." She hugs and kisses her daughter and then walks over to the set, stopping to hug crew members and engaging in happy banter with an enthusiasm that belies the fact that she said goodbye to these people only two months ago.

But it is not all idle gossip. Much had happened during the show's hiatus. Duchovny had used his time off to do a movie, *Playing God*, in which he played a mob doctor. James Wong and Glenn Morgan, who had left at the end of the second season to pilot the fortunes of their own creation, *Space: Above and Beyond*, had unfortunately seen their baby fall victim to low ratings. Wong and Morgan, now back in the *X-Files* fold, were already credited with two of the early batch of new scripts. And finally, the long-rumored *X-Files* movie has become a reality. Chris Carter is nearing the finish line on a completed script, and the film is slated to be shot in the spring of 1997. Carter will only hint that the movie "will be a scary, stand-alone story that will not in any way alter *The X-Files'* TV story lines."

Anderson, for her part, describes her vacation away from the series this way. "I went to Italy, France, Munich, Bali and Tahiti, Los Angeles, and New York City. It was part vacation and part business. I know it doesn't sound like there was much rest involved in all of that, but there was, in fact, a good deal of rest along the way. I got a good week here and a good week there with no promotional stuff involved at all."

Anderson, in these early days back, seems reinvigorated by the hiatus, having stretched her wings on some outside projects and radiating confidence that her next break from the show will leave her time for even more opportunities. "I would love to do a comedy," she exclaims. "If something like that came up, or even a small role in a big feature, I'd do that."

Much of Anderson's good spirits have to do with Piper's continuing to be a constant, positive focus in her life. The actress appears to have found the perfect balance between career and motherhood, and the realization that she can have it all radiates out in a constant smile and general good cheer even under the most trying *X-Files* conditions.

Anderson is particularly happy that the more revealing, personal details that came out during the hiatus have not gotten in the way of her growing celebrity status. "To be perfectly honest, I'm at the point where I don't want to hear any more revelations about my past," she admits, no doubt, in response to the firestorm ignited by her revealing interview in *For Him Magazine*. "Everything I've said is true, but a lot of it has been blown up into something that I never expected it to be. Time and again, people have asked me about the punk phase I went through. I've maybe told them a sentence or two about it and the press has blown it up and centered their articles on that period of my life. It wasn't something I necessarily wanted to talk about beyond the first one or two times I talked about it. I know it's interesting to some people, but isn't it old news now?" She reflects, "On the whole, my work continues to be very separate from my private life. In any case, it's the work that ultimately counts, and the nature of my work doesn't really allow me to focus on much else."

The X-Files, entering its fourth season, has demanded most of Anderson's time and energy. She still seems in awe of the show's success. "I have no idea how we made it this far. How did this happen? It just blows me away. I think, in the beginning, we all pretty much felt we would do one season and that would be it. The fact that we're still here has got to be the most shocking thing of all."

The show's popularity has proved a mixed blessing. Anderson admits to craving the success, but she is dismayed about the price the notoriety is having on her personal life, which she continues to guard with bulldog tenacity. The hard work continues to take its toll both physically and emotionally. Throw in the additional pressures of being a wife and mother and it is no wonder that Anderson is occasionally overwhelmed. "It's all strange, just very strange," she chuckled during a recent break on the set. "I don't even have a real handle on how strange it is. I've just accepted that it's strange and just try to go with the flow. I show up for whatever happens, and I tend not to think about this stuff too much in retrospect or take too much of it too seriously or personally. Fame and the popularity of the show are just what they are, and I'm doing my best to deal with them."

Anderson's high-publicity summer, which featured her Australian visit, seems to have sharpened her sense of fame and how she's handling it. And given recent remarks, it sounds as though she's handling it like the seasoned veteran she's become. "The obligations of fame are interesting," she offers. "I remember the period of time when I was pregnant, when it really hit me that the show was getting successful, that I felt a responsibility to the audience to maintain at a time when I couldn't maintain because I was pregnant, tired, and just going through the whole hormonal thing. That was the first time any obligation really hit me. No fan of *X-Files* wants to hear me bitch about my life or the fans. So I try very hard, these days, to maintain a positive frame of mind about everything."

With the new season has come a new round of rumors, and Anderson can only laugh and say, "Where does this stuff come from?" One rumor has Mulder being killed off and replaced by a character from the TV series *Babylon 5*. Another has both Mulder and Scully disappearing under mysterious circumstances and being replaced in their roles by Skinner, Mr. X, and The Lone Gunmen. Carter, with no small sense of seriousness in his voice, says don't hold your breath. "I've never thought of it. I've never had to consider it. If the time came, I would deal with it, but I hope the time never comes."

Playing along with the rampant speculation, the actress offers up her own idea of an outrageous *X-Files* story line. "I think it would be great for something romantic to happen between Scully and Skinner," she smirks. "But I've read a couple of interviews in which Chris has said that won't happen. So I assume it won't."

Carter, giving away nothing, does tease that at some point in the new season, "Mulder will see something he thinks is paranormal, and Scully will say no it can't be. Like all good *X-Files* episodes, these shows will pose more questions than they answer."

One *X-Files* rumor with a bit more substance to it is that Duchovny has demanded that Carter give Mulder a girlfriend this season. Carter, in interviews, has not ruled out the actor's request. Duchovny, as angry as he ever gets, says, "That's bullshit! Yes, I would like to have some kind of personal life and an obvious way to do that is to have some kind of love interest. But Chris gets scared and puts it on my shoulders. I bridle at the perception of myself as some kind of Frankenstein asking for a bride."

Anderson seems to have come to grips with the reality and the grind of the show, but she did succumb to a bad case of foot in mouth in an interview conducted in early 1996. In a state of distraction, she offered an unfortunate description of working on *The X-Files*. "It's like a death sentence."

In the same interview, Anderson expressed some concern about how long the show could keep up its high quality. "I'm praying to God that it won't go another four years. You have to wonder how long they can continue to pull off these original scripts. After a while, they're going to have to start pulling from old ideas, and everyone is going to be comparing this episode to that one. I hope they have the sense to pull out before the show gets stale."

When Carter got wind of Anderson's comments, he was clearly offended by her likening the show to a "death sentence." "I was upset," he acknowledges. "I called her and said, 'Look, this is the chance of a lifetime. The work is so hard, I'm sure you feel as if you've signed your life away. But, if we all felt like that, we might as well go home and pack it up.'"

Anderson backpedaled after the conversation with Carter. "It was a meaningless joke," she said by way of an apology. "I felt bad for the people it affected and so, from now on, I'm being careful."

It is not known for sure how much Carter's admonishment affected Anderson's willingness to talk candidly. But, in ensuing interviews, the actress, while continuing to pepper her conversation with subtle stabs of humor, did appear to be guarded and considerably less open. When contract renegotiations gave her more money but added two years to her commitment to the show, a reporter asked Anderson if she was ready for that much Scully. The actress cautiously replied, "I don't know if anybody is. You take it one year at a time."

"I didn't foresee at all that the show was going to be as popular as it is," Anderson admits. "Now my body and psyche are used to it, but I still can't fathom what we might go into in year five or year six. I can't even think about that because I start to panic."

Anderson, always quick to praise the show's writers in the past, began to take an even more admiring stance toward their efforts. "Sometimes I look at the scripts and think 'What were they on when they came up with that idea? And how in the hell are we going to pull that off?' But we always do and that says a lot for their talent and imagination."

"Herrenvolk," which kicked off *The*

X-Files' fourth season, was primarily a Mulder episode. The concluding segment of the previous season's cliff-hanger found the agent encountering, in a sense, his long-lost sister and dealing with his mother, who was on her deathbed. Anderson's participation took a backseat, her scenes with Skinner and a lot of chasing around being the high points. Some rumormongers were quick to suggest that Carter and the writers were giving her a slap on the wrist for her previous negative comments about the show. Anderson, however, was quick to laugh off that theory and reverted to extolling the virtues of each and every script that comes her way. "The scripts continue to lay out the degree of emotions that we're allowed to express," she offers. "This show requires more of an emotional commitment and more technical work from an acting standpoint."

Anderson had quite a bit more to chew on in the season's second episode, "Home," in which Mulder and Scully, while investigating a family of small-town genetic mutants, have a telling conversation on a park bench about their families' respective genetic makeups. Mulder even speculates on Scully's maternal future, at one point jokingly referring to Scully as "mom." She responds with a powerful look that manages to reveal both Scully's inner hopes and dreams as well as some insight into Anderson, the real-life mother.

Journalists continue to pepper Anderson with questions reminiscent of the halcyon days of the show's first two seasons. Once they get past the inevitable speculation of a Mulder-Scully romance, the one question that often seems to surface is how long she believes *The X-Files* should run. "I'd be happy for it to go on as long as it needs to go," she responds. "I'm sure that, if it goes that long, the sixth and seventh seasons will be grueling. I just hope that it is allowed to end when it needs to end and that it's not pushed beyond its expectations."

In the meantime, filming the episode "Unrhue," a grisly bit of business about a troubled man who has taken to lobotomizing women with an ice pick, entails more thrills and chills for Scully. Scully has been captured by the psycho and, under the direction of Rob Bowman, is literally under the knife as Mulder races against time to save the brain of his partner. It's an emotionally tough exercise for Anderson, who, as take upon take piles up, is alternating between moments of fear and tough determination. This, in essence, is Scully coming full circle. "I guess my character has come into her own," Anderson comments. "The scripts are allowing me to be very real and believable, which means I get to be strong and I get to be scared."

Anderson, when she has a moment to spare in this early burst to get episodes in the can prior to the October 4 season premiere, is playing it coy about the upcoming season, revealing only enough to tease. "Some words will pass between Mulder and Scully that have never been hinted at before," she chuckles. "We also have an episode called 'Home,' which is probably one of the most bizarre things we've ever done. It's about a strange family in a little town. They have no electricity and no heat, and they've been breeding their own cattle, pigs, chickens, and even their own family."

The actress has begun to also address, albeit in vague terms, her post-*X-Files* plans. She continues to insist that the *X-Files* motion picture is a question mark at best and offers that she is considering some movie scripts that would "take me very far away from anything like *X-Files*."

Anderson has also done a bit of backtracking on previous statements that producing was in her future. "I know I said those things," she admits, "but I'm not really interested in producing anymore. But I definitely like the idea of creative input. Now that things have balanced out a bit and I have a few more minutes here and there, I've had a bit more time to put some of my ideas on paper." The actress was doing more than speculating, however. She has since met with Carter for the specific purpose of bouncing her ideas off him, and Carter was high enough on one to pencil it in as a definite go sometime in the near future.

"The nominations for Lead Actress in a Drama Series are Kathy Baker for *Picket Fences*, Christine Lahti for *Chicago Hope*, Angela Lansbury for *Murder, She Wrote*, Sherry Stringfield for *ER*, and Gillian Anderson for *The X-Files*."

The July 1996 Emmy announcements were a decidedly mixed bag for *The X-Files*.

The show garnered eight nominations, with Anderson's best actress and the show's best drama heading the list. Many were dismayed that Duchovny, in an admittedly crowded field, did not make the final cut for best actor. Duchovny, though never a big believer in awards to start with, suggested the slight was "a confusing omission." Carter, a firm believer in team play, viewed the nominations as a mixed blessing. "I felt bad for David," he says. "I think the tendency with this show is to see Gillian and David in competition with each other. You can't look at it that way, and, unfortunately, when something like these nominations happens, it tends to blow something up that is not really true."

Anderson was happy to get the news but took it in stride. "I guess I'll have to spend ten minutes a day practicing my 'It's an honor to be nominated' look," she laughs, "because you never know when a camera will be on you. To be perfectly honest, I think this is the Angela Lansbury award. But I will put something down on paper and place it under my left cheek, and hopefully I'll get to use it. Seriously, I'm very excited and honored, but at the end of the day, it ultimately comes down to the work."

As the Emmy Awards loomed on the horizon, Anderson found the nomination a compliment and, occasionally, a good-natured curse. On a particularly difficult shooting day, in a scene with Mitch Pileggi and a lot of extras, Anderson was having a rough time with some scientific babble. After the latest in an uncharacteristic series of flubs, Pileggi turned to the extras and announced, "Ladies and gentlemen, this performance is courtesy of the Emmy-nominated Gillian Anderson." Anderson let loose with a profanity in the direction of Pileggi and then dissolved into laughter.

As the fourth season continued to progress, Anderson, in contrast with costar Duchovny's insistence on doing only the minimal amount of publicity required by his contract, found time to really immerse herself in the talk-show circuit. She made a second appearance on *The Late Show with David Letterman*, where her sense of class and no-nonsense attitude reduced the notoriously lazy (when it comes to research and treatment of guests) Letterman to a babbling caricature of a talk-show host. She was also able to bat the softballs tossed her way by the newly crowned queen of talk-show banter, Rosie O'Donnell.

Anderson's media profile could not have been higher, but those television appearances reignited the latest flurry of rumors that her three-year-old marriage was in trouble. On both shows, the absence of her wedding ring was conspicuous. And, despite her insistence in recent interviews that she and Klotz were "quite happy," Anderson, in a moment of candor, indicated that her newfound star status was, in fact, putting unreasonable pressures on their relationship. "There's no reason why it should but it does," she says with more than a little irritation in her voice at the constant prying. "Anybody in the situation I'm in right now would be a difficult partner."

As often accompanies a meteoric rise to stardom, an interest developed in Anderson's early work just as the fourth season of *The X-Files* began to unfold. It was not *The Turning* that had finally surfaced but rather an Internet announcement that *A Matter of Choice*, with William Davis's permission, was being made available in a very limited edition of 250 copies on a first-come, first-served basis.

For even the most fanatic of *X-Files* viewers, the existence of this film, which had gone on to capture a Chicago-area experimental film award in 1988, was real news—the reason being that Anderson, in her myriad of interviews, had never indicated such a project even existed. One can only speculate that though Anderson might defend *A Matter of Choice* as a quality piece of acting, her handlers were most likely advising her that fans might be offended to learn of her involvement in a controversial pro-choice project.

Southern California in early September can be rough on formal wear. Traditionally the last gasp of summer, temperatures regularly soar past the high 90s and into the low triple digits. Hot isn't the word for it. Uncomfortable is.

And uncomfortable is what it was that midafternoon when the limo carrying Gillian Anderson cruised off the Pasadena Freeway, down Colorado Boulevard, and turned a sharp right, heading for the Pasadena Civic Auditorium, where the Emmy Award ceremonies were about to commence. It had been a rough night for Gillian, her apprehensive state erupting, by morning, into a case of full-blown nerves. Small talk turned into no talk as the limo neared its destination.

The limo pulled to a stop outside the auditorium. To her right was a seemingly mile-long red carpet that would usher her into the ceremonies. Gillian, in a glamorous gown complemented by an un-Scully-like hairstyle, exited the limo.

"Look! It's Gillian! Gillian, we love you! Gillian! Gillian! Over here!"

Anderson looked in the direction of a long grandstand sitting in front of the nearby mall directly across the street. Fans of all ages were shouting and going bananas at the mere sight of her. This level of hysteria was no longer new to her, but the intensity of their devotion coupled with her case of nerves gave her a shudder. She smiled and waved in the direction of the fans. But the look on her face told the true story.

Gillian Anderson was scared to death.

Anderson entered the auditorium and

sat down near the front of the stage. She was trying to be cool, but she couldn't help but crane her neck when George Clooney, Christine Lahti, and other stars walked down the aisle. In another life she might have gone up to them and asked for an autograph. But in a very big sense, Gillian Anderson was now in their league.

The awards ceremony began and quickly settled into a predictable agenda of thank you speeches and amazed and, if you looked quickly, disappointed looks on the faces of the winners and losers. About midway through the show, Anderson was summoned backstage and met with her copresenter prior to their presenting one of the awards.

With background music welling up, Anderson and her copresenter were ushered onto the stage and over to the podium. Anderson was visibly nervous, her eyes wide and her voice slightly quivering, as she stared toward the TelePrompTer that offered up the introductory comments and the nominees. The winner announced, Anderson moves off the stage and back to her seat. She calms down a bit but continues to shift uncomfortably in her seat.

"The nominees for best actress in a drama series are . . ."

Anderson appears on camera as her name is announced. Her smile is tense, but then for a moment a look of confidence appears on her face. One could sense that Anderson felt she had a chance of winning.

"And the winner is . . . Kathy Baker!"

A flash of visible disappointment transformed Gillian Anderson's face before she joined in applauding Baker's victory.

As the crowd filed slowly out of the Pasadena Civic, the sun was slowly beginning its early evening descent. Anderson, following the conclusion of the ceremony, gave a few perfunctory quotes to reporters before heading for her waiting limo. The fans from the stands had, for the most part, departed before the show let out. But a handful of diehards remained.

"We love you Gillian! We love you!"

Anderson seemed to finally relax at that point, acknowledging the fans with a very real smile and wave. She stepped inside her limo, which pulled out and headed toward the freeway that would take her back to the other side of town for a quick stop in at a post-Emmy party or two and finally back to her hotel. She's allowed only a few hours' sleep before catching a plane back to Vancouver and starting another hellish sixteen-hour day on the show that had snatched her from obscurity and had put her name on the world's lips. "Sometimes *X-Files* seems like forever," Anderson muses. "It's only in retrospect, when I read about other people's paths, that I realize how lucky I've been."

Anderson's thoughts drifted to her husband and her daughter as early evening Los Angeles raced past her limo window. There were still many questions that needed to be answered, and what would happen when *The X-Files* finally ended was anybody's guess. But the future looked bright. No, she did not win the Emmy.

But Gillian Anderson was truly a winner this night.

Gillian Anderson and Clyde Klotz's three-year marriage ended January 1997 with the official announcement that the couple had agreed to "an amicable separation." The British tabloid *The Sun*, who reported that Klotz had moved out of the couple's Vancouver home in October, said Klotz took care of Piper over the Christmas holidays while Anderson, in the company of a "young man," spent Christmas in London.

eleven

SCULLY SAYS WHAT?

OVER THE COURSE OF THE PAST THREE YEARS, Gillian Anderson has been the recipient of some of the most hilarious, often tongue-in-cheek dialogue to ever grace a dramatic series. What follows is a random sampling of the wit and wisdom of Agent Dana Scully. Taken totally out of context, of course.

āTHE X-FILESā

Agent Mulder believes we are not alone.

The answers are there. You just have to know where to look for them.

äSPACEä

It's an oxygen leak. Even I can figure out what happens when they run out of oxygen.

äSQUEEZEä

Oh God, Mulder! It smells like . . . I think it's bile!

äMIRACLE MANä

A few dozen grasshoppers does not constitute a plague.

äTHE JERSEY DEVILä

Mulder? He's a jerk!

Keep it up, Mulder, and I'll hurt you like that beast woman.

äSHADOWSä

Psycho Kinesis? You mean how Carrie got even at the prom?

äGENDERBENDERä

So what is our profile of the killer? Intermediate height, weight, sex, unarmed but extremely attractive.

äDARKNESS FALLSä

Oh, brain-sucking parasites.

äTOOMSä

Mulder, it's getting a little ripe in here, don't you think?

äROLANDä

You mean the part where the groom passed out or the dog bit the drummer?

By the look of this, he's hamburger.

äTHE ERLENMEYER FLASKä

If this is monkey pee, you're on your own.

äHOSTä

Maybe you'd rather hear what you can catch from a nice rare steak.

äBLOODä

Mulder, I was wrong. Exposure to insecticide does induce paranoia.

äDUANE BARRYä

I'm not going to calm down until I can talk to someone who will listen to what I'm saying.

äIRRESISTIBLEä

It took us three hours to get here and our plane doesn't leave until tomorrow night.

äDIE HAND DIE VERLETZTä

Mulder! Toads just fell out of the sky.

äFRESH BONESä

Maybe I should kiss a few and find out if one is Guitterez.

äDPOä

Mulder, what's that in your pocket?

äCLYDE BRUCKMAN'S FINAL REPOSEä

Sorry, I didn't mean to give off any negative energy.

äOUBLIETTEä

I hate to say this, Mulder, but I think you just ran out of credibility.

äREVELATIONSä

Would you do me a favor? Would you smell Mr. Jarvis?

āPUSHERä

Please explain to me the scientific nature of the whammy.

āJOSÉ CHUNG'S 'FROM OUTER SPACE' ä

So we know that it wasn't an alien that probed her.

That was Detective Manners. He said they just found your bleeping UFO.

āQUAGMIREä

His fly's undone.

āWET WIREDä

You're one of them!

twelve

CATCH A WAVE

GILLIAN ANDERSON HAS BECOME A DARLING OF THE information superhighway, an Internet charmer who has become the topic of perpetual rumor, speculation, fantasy, and adoration on an intellectual and physical level. And Anderson has been quite happy with this unique form of adulation. "I'm flattered that the people who have taken to Scully tend to be the computer guys," she offers. "I actually enjoy that I don't get the typical fan letters from people saying, 'Oh, you're so beautiful, I want to marry you, I can't wait until you take your clothes off.' Oh sure, there's some of that on the computer, but there's a certain degree of intelligence that goes along with the computer people."

Now that you've heard the whole story, I'd like to recommend the following computer web sites and forums as your ticket to ride the ongoing odyssey of everybody's favorite *X-Files* charmer.

THE X-FILES FORUM

Typing X-Files on your screen and clicking on the mysterious figure under the phrase *Trust No One* allows you to gain admission to more than one hundred discussion boards centering on all kinds of *X-Files* and Gillian Anderson rumors, facts and fantasies, and wishful thinking. But there's more to the forum than mere chat. An extensive *X-Files* archive chronicles convention transcripts, Gillian Anderson photos, and lots of print and radio interviews.

THE GILLIAN ANDERSON HOME PAGE

A solid primer to the Gillian Anderson phenomenon, this home page includes frequently asked questions, print interviews, and radio transcripts of Anderson inter-

views, and a jumping-off point to other Gillian Anderson pages.
http://duggy.extern.ucsd.edu/%7
elinny/Gillian.html

ANOTHER GILLIAN ANDERSON HOME PAGE (AKA MULDER . . . IT'S ME)

Easily the best Gillian Anderson home page on the Net! This constantly updated page consists of newspaper and magazine interview transcripts and articles, sound bites, and additional Anderson pages and photo sites. I've seen newspaper stories on Anderson hit this page within forty-eight hours of the media appearance. This is the place to go for that daily fix.
http://cygnus.rsabbs.com/kwitzig/
gillian.html

THE GILLIAN ANDERSON TESTOSTERONE BRIGADE

Though this chat site will occasionally make mention of Gillian Anderson's brains, it's her body that this largely male on-line group is interested in. The missives run the gamut from worshipful to downright raunchy.
http://www.bchs.uh.edu/=ecantu/GATB

THE GILLIAN ANDERSON PHOTO GALLERY

A feast for the eyes, this photo extravaganza brings more than two hundred scanned photos of Anderson at various points in her career into sharp focus.
http://www.proxy.aol.com

GILLIAN'S ISLAND

It was inevitable that a web site dedicated to the more goofy aspects of the *X-Files*–Gillian Anderson phenomenon would emerge and this is it. This funhouse contains some hilarious sound bites, off-the-wall interview clips, and an *X-Files* Christmas special spoof featuring the willing voices of Anderson and Duchovny.
http://www.blarg.net/miri/xf/ga/rwreed/scully=page.html

SCULLY: A DISCUSSION OF THE PHOTOGRAPHIC JOURNEY OF GILLIAN ANDERSON

A pretty straightforward photo history of Gillian Anderson, focusing on Anderson in front of the camera and featuring a studious, well-informed audio narration, which, among other things, debunks the rumored

nude photos of Anderson that are reportedly making the rounds on the Internet.
http://home.earthlink.net

GO GILLIAN ANDERSON

Some alleged former schoolmates of Gillian Anderson have set up this site to chronicle memories of her wonder years. Lots of quotes talking about her wild life and teen years. Updated on a fairly regular basis.
http://shoga.wwa.com/=phlash/goga.html

CHURCH OF THE IMMACULATE GILLIAN

Totally tongue-in-cheek. Visit the Gillian Anderson shrine. Read a sermon. Make a sacrifice. Good clean fun.
http://www.hway.net/ggc/cig.html

THE GILLIAN ANDERSON ESTROGEN BRIGADE

The flip side of the Testosterone Brigade, this web site offers a forum for women who admire Anderson for nonsexist reasons.
http://207.86.129.202/gaeb/

THE GENUINE ADMIRERS OF GILLIAN ANDERSON ASSOCIATION

The denizens of this web site dig Gillian Anderson for her skills as an actress and for being a wonderful wife and mother. Praise for all the right reasons dwells here. http://www.cyberbeach.net/-jonmg/GA/GAGA.html